Heard

by

Suzanne Jefferies

Heard

Contact Information: info@thewildrosepress.com

Cover Art by *Debbie Taylor*

The Wild Rose Press, Inc.
PO Box 708
Adams Basin, NY 14410-0708

Visit us at www.thewildrosepress.com

Publishing History
First Scarlet Rose Edition, 2020
Print ISBN 978-1-5092-2948-2
Digital ISBN 978-1-5092-2949-9

Published in the United States of America

In her darkness, he's her light...

He closes the space between us. A big man, with long strides, heavy boots? Yeah, this was a boot man, all right. I'd take a bet he was wearing well-worn jeans too.

He touches the grocery bag, pulling it toward him, tentative. "Let me take those from you."

Close to me, he smells deliciously spicy, musky, all the things I haven't smelled up close for two years. I feel for the handrail, and step upward.

"No, wait." He's firm.

I pause.

"I'll take you up first, then come back for your things."

Have I heard him right? "Take me up first?"

"Carry you up, ma'am."

I correct him. "Skye."

Carry me up? Carry me up six flights of stairs? Part of me wants to say, hell no, what do I look like, an invalid? The other part? Throb, throb, throb. That ankle makes its answer known. "Sure. If you don't think you'll break your back or something. I can't promise that there won't be pain tomorrow."

"There won't be."

Mr. Confidence on full strength. Well, he offered. I hold onto the rail while he takes each crutch from me. Then, with one fluid motion, he sweeps me up into his arms. Quick feet ease up those stairs.

Dedication

To my ROSA coffee club ladies
who keep me going when I want to give up.

Chapter One

"Elevator's out again." His voice is thick, shot through with a southern twang.

It's a voice I haven't heard before. I tilt my head a little. "Yeah? That's the third time this month already."

"Fourth."

He hasn't approached me. There's only the slightest movement, a shift of weight, perhaps. "Guess it's the stairs then." I readjust the crutches under my armpits. Only a week or so, and it's *adios* to the cast, the crutches, the whole how-to-slow-you-down starter kit. My groceries slap against my thighs as I turn and begin the nine paces to the stairwell.

"You want I should give you a hand with that?"

There's nothing in his voice to suggest menace. Still, his voice is one I don't know, and am not familiar with.

A clawed feet pitter-patter trots up from the ground floor passageway. I brace for the onslaught of bustling woman and dog. "Morning, Mrs. Adams."

But she's on today's mission. "Rogan? You're the super's nephew, right? Now I've got a blocked drain that's keeping me up all night."

Interesting. Do I detect a note of flirtation? Mrs. Adams—who heads up the schnauzer appreciation club and whose own schnauzer is appreciating my grocery bag, her nose snuffling up close and personal into the

1

plastic—is flirting with the super's nephew.

"Yes, ma'am, I'll be right on it."

"Not now, come by later, gotta get Cherry Jubilee her treats now. But I'll be back by six."

I smile at that. Who knew that Mrs. Adams could play coquette? The super's nephew must be pretty super himself.

I make my way toward the stairs as the building's glass door clangs shut, sucking Mrs. Adams into the wide world outside. Six whole flights up and counting. What's that they say about every great journey starting with a single step?

"You're sure I can't help you out?"

He moves now, a little closer to me. My ankle may be this close to healed, but right now, it throbs in its plaster tomb. Lug it and these grocery bags up six flights? I hesitate.

"That sure looks heavy."

It sure is.

Maybe it's because he hasn't inched forward but stuck his ground, waiting for my go-ahead. Maybe it's because he hasn't layered meaning into those words. Maybe it's because sometimes you've gotta believe that people can be helpful, friendly, caring, and all those good things. Either way, I agree. "I'm on the sixth floor."

"No problem, ma'am."

"It's Skye."

He closes the space between us. A big man, with long strides, heavy boots? Yeah, this was a boot man, all right. I'd take a bet he was wearing well-worn jeans too.

He touches the grocery bag, pulling it toward him,

tentative. "Let me take those from you."

Close to me, he smells deliciously spicy, musky, all the things I haven't smelled up close for two years. I feel for the handrail, and step upward.

"No, wait." He's firm.

I pause.

"I'll take you up first, then come back for your things."

Have I heard him right? "Take me up first?"

"Carry you up, ma'am."

I correct him. "Skye."

Carry me up? Carry me up six flights of stairs? Part of me wants to say, hell no, what do I look like, an invalid? The other part? Throb, throb, throb. That ankle makes its answer known. "Sure. If you don't think you'll break your back or something. I can't promise that there won't be pain tomorrow."

"There won't be."

Mr. Confidence on full strength. Well, he offered. I hold onto the rail while he takes each crutch from me. Then, with one fluid motion, he sweeps me up into his arms. Quick feet ease up those stairs.

I'm right. He's tall, over six feet at least. And broad. Solid, dense-packed muscle stretches over his broad chest, and his abdomen is rock-hard. I drape my arm over his shoulders, enjoying those arm muscles' bumpedy-bump ripple. His heart beats close to me, but his breathing remains calm and even. A fit man. Correction—an incredibly fit man, no doubt one of those who never skips a gym session, even with full-blown flu.

Kevin, the super—his uncle—is short, squat, and breathes with the help of an oxygen machine that he carts about. No wonder Mrs. Adams had turned up the heat.

Something jangles around his neck, something metallic. I'd guess dog tags. Considering the body, the clipped short-speak style and the prodigious use of 'ma'am', the super's nephew must be out on military leave or something.

Please don't let him be military.

"Which is yours?"

So soon? This guy never misses leg day, that's for sure. "The one with the white door." That's how Ma describes it. A white door for me is a memory of a white door that I saw before—a wooden, paneled affair painted slick in white gloss. Our door is not paneled and is made up of plywood. It's smooth with an unremarkable finish and a standard handle. Even the numbering is regulation built. But the memory sticks.

He slows a little as he nears flat 604.

Curiously, I'm disappointed. Cradled in his arms, close to his male warmspice, a melancholic pang of loneliness rises up. Once upon a time, I'd imagined this. To be held close, like this. The memory stirs up something long forgotten, and I push it back down again.

He lets me down, careful not to knock the plastered foot.

Is it my imagination or is the moving apart of our bodies slower than I'd expect? Of course it's my imagination. Too long without anyone close, that's all. A silent scream at the lack of touch in my life echoes from inside. I can hear it—I can always hear it.

I fumble for my key, all business.

His voice intrudes. "I'll go get your things." His

presence—so rich, so full, so calm—recedes as he heads back down the passage.

It's an ache in my gut. *What?* I open the door and hop into the apartment I share with my mother. It's small, clean, and purely functional. There's simply not enough money for it to be anything better. And empty. Thank God, Ma won't be back for hours yet.

I lean against the wall and wait for his return.

What did Mrs. Adams say his name was? Rogan? Is that *Mr.* Rogan or his first name? Did he suit his name? A strong-sounding name, certainly a strong man. Was he blond or dark? A redhead, even? And his skin color? Olive, pale, or rich dark? And his eyes? What color did the light reflect? Blue, green, brown, or shades in-between?

Ah, but even if I know these details, I can't piece them together in my head. Not anymore.

His boots echo along the passageway as he returns.

I smooth and pat my hair, making sure it's all in place.

"Here. Your crutches."

I reach forward, connecting with my temporary leg substitutes. "Thank you."

"Where can I put this down?"

I guess he means my reason for being out and about that morning. Picking up groceries after my weekly meeting. It's been two years now and I still go, even though the danger's not as urgent as it once was. But I guess that's today. Tomorrow or even next month, things could be different again.

"The kitchen, please." I gesture toward the kitchenette and the empty counter. "Can I get you something to drink? Coffee? Water?"

The bags connect with the counter. "I'll take some water, please, ma'am."

"Skye. It's Skye…and you are?"

"Chase Rogan."

That solves that mystery. "Filling in for your uncle, is that right?"

There's a silence. Did he nod? Or shake his head? Or simply not answer my question?

I swing around into the kitchen, find a glass, and fill it with cold water from the fridge. "You like some ice with that?"

"No, thank you…Skye."

Better than ma'am. I hold out the glass to where he's waiting.

His breathing is slow and steady, in through his nose, then soft out of his mouth. No gulping for air with greedy grasps or whistling through sinus passages.

It still surprises me—the differences in how people breathe. I can tell a lot about people from the way they suck up their oxygen. Chase Rogan's exhale is long and measured. From a man who worked out hard. If I hadn't known it from the way he scaled those stairs, I'd know it from that super-long almost sigh. Sexy.

He takes the glass from me, his fingers lightly brushing against mine.

A slight awakening of something deep inside me starts to unsettle. It's been so long since a man touched me at all. Even if only by accident.

A gulp as he swallows. He's close enough that I can smell that warmspice of him. Aftershave? Or him. I swallow as I consider the latter.

I run my hand over the counter to where he's put my grocery bags. "You think they'll be able to get the elevator fixed sooner rather than later?" My scrambling around for conversation topics is similar to my rummaging through my purchases. Fingers all thumbs, I pull out broccoli and celery, and barely register their sharp scent. "You like broccoli? I make a mean chicken-and-broccoli pie."

Since when did I become Mrs. Adams? Oh, about ten minutes or so ago when a man I'd never met before swept me off my feet and carried me to my door. Did that really happen? He closes the space between us, and his larger, steadier hand rests over mine. My mouth dries, and my heart races a little faster than it should.

"Let me help you with that."

"It's okay, I got it." I swipe away the eggs, feeling the tray bend slightly toward the floor. Holy shit. The last thing I need is to drop the eggs. Icky, sticky, slick mess. And yet, that image conjures up thoughts that my brain has no right to magic up—with this stranger who's standing in my mother's kitchen drinking water in measured gulps. Icky, sticky, slick mess with the stranger who smells so good, I want to bathe in him.

He steps away a fraction.

I concentrate on my task—opening cupboards, loading cans, stacking things in the fridge. Pack away all thoughts of this man with the hard abs and the kind voice—was that voice kind? Yes. It speaks of warmth and empathy. *Losing it, I was losing it.* That's what a few months of recuperating with a broken ankle did. It had scrambled my brains and rearranged my senses. That's what was going on.

Barely moving, he stretches over to the sink, rinses out the glass, sets it out on the draining board.

Please don't go. The words flash through me.

He drawls. "If you need to head back out, you can call for me."

It's been a while, but I can feel that heat in my cheeks rising as inevitable as the sun in the west. "That's very nice of you to offer."

"Can't have you...up and down those stairs."

My voice chirps in response—there's not a lick sexy about it. "It's a week or so and then the cast is off, and I'll be good to go."

"Yeah, I noticed that the stopper on your one crutch is a little loose. You want me to have a look at it? Only take a minute."

"Sure." Any second now and my blush would self-combust. "Maybe let me sit first?"

I'm aware of him behind me, the space he fills as he follows me into the lounge. I find the couch, drop into it, and automatically, raise my ankle onto the coffee table. "So stupid of me, I tripped over Mrs. Adams's dog in the hall. My fault, should have known better."

He's not big on large movement. There's no restlessness in that body. Still calm.

Were it not for that deliciousness wafting from him, I'd barely be aware of his presence. And yet, all I'm aware of is his presence. It's as if he's filling up the entire room. I could swim in him, just let myself sink down, down, down, into him deep, deep, deep.

A smacking sound reminds me that I'm sitting on my couch with the super's nephew fixing my crutch. Ah, but for a second, I felt that stirring that—

"All done."

"Thank you."

A slight pause. "I can let myself out."

Attendez. "Wait." I stop him. Never have I so understood the desire to hold someone's attention, to have them attend to me. Is that not what waiting is? A focused attention on one person as they complete their business?

"May I?" I gesture with my hands over my face. "It's good to know who I'm talking to."

Another pause. "Yes, ma'…Skye. Sure. Where do you want me?"

I bite back the answer that springs to mind— everywhere. I want this stranger, everywhere. I slap the seat next to me.

He perches.

I find his arm and squeeze slightly. "It'll only take a second."

He doesn't flinch as I move my fingers over his face. I'm still not a pro at this. It's taken time. But my fingers join up some of the dots that my eyes used to. This close to him, his musky raw scent nearly undoes me. It's not aftershave—it's him, all right. No commercial-made product could match that, the layers underneath, the throb as it pulses from him. Was he even aware of how good he smells? If I could bury myself in his neck, his chest, everywhere. *I want him everywhere.* His scent floods my nose, triggering off wave after wave of desire. I take a deep breath and read him.

My fingertips flutter across his skin.

His stubble is a few days' worth and heavy at that. His jaw is hard, square, and finishes in a cleft in his chin. From the way the muscles are set, this is a guy who likes to clamp down hard on his anger.

I bet he grinds his teeth in his sleep.

So much wire and tension in that jaw. All that pent-up energy with nowhere to go but in. His lips are full and perfectly even. There are deep furrows where his eyebrows meet—this guy's spent some time squinting at the sun.

Thick eyebrows frame his eyes, and his lashes brush against me. No way this guy is blond. Coupled with that heavy stubble, I'd go with dark on dark. Your classic tall, dark, and handsome mysterious stranger.

I find the scar that gouges his cheek and his face muscles tense.

But he doesn't move away.

"Nice to meet you, Mr. Rogan." The polite tone belies the churning in my belly. Why can't I be one of those women who has the quick lines, the witty repartee that would let him know in no uncertain terms how much I want to slide his clothes off of him and curl up on his warm, so warm, body.

And yet, I'm embarrassed that that's what I want to do—no getting to know, or idle chitchat, just the nuts and bolts of body parts moving together until they erupt in pleasure.

He finds my hand and squeezes it in a handshake.

That squeeze replicates in my core, a clamping down of lust that's seeping up in me. His handshake's firm and dry, and that heat is in his palms, as his hand traps mine, holding it that fraction longer than necessary.

I work my fingers over his hand, tracing the patterns of his past that are etched in deep. Rough hands with sandpaper edges. A man who works with his hands. Older hands. No young nephew here. I'd go with mid-thirties, maybe later? The boldness of my move catches me unaware. It's as if I'm observing myself from a distance, as I gently grip each of his fingers, sliding them through mine, each and every ridge of bone and sinew telling its own story. I could stop, probably should stop. But his scent has invaded me, enveloping me, beckoning me closer. There's no ring on his fingers; his baby finger's nail is bitten down to the quick. And a tense jaw. An anxious man. What have his eyes seen? What have his hands been involved with?

Please don't let him be military. Anything but military.

I flip his hand over, and work over his open palm, over the fleshy ball of his thumb. When I was much younger, around sixteen or so, I'd read a book on palmistry as a potential party trick. And, now, here I am so many years later, no wiser, but still desperate to read a person's past, their future, in the lines of their hands. Does that fleshy part equal a lusty nature? Or the betrayal of the womanizer? And his heart line? Does it promise passion? Or a long life?

My mind scratches about, failing to snatch up bits of memory. Why am I chasing the past, when the present is unrolling in front of me? Maybe it's that unrolling that's causing my thoughts to scatter so. His hand is in mine, and he hasn't moved it away as I continue my slow exploration. His breathing is slow and steady, lulling me into a calm that I swear I'm making up. He's seen my eyes…how they stare out at nothing. He's indulging me.

And yet.

I reach the tender part of his wrist, where the blood flows much hotter, where the skin is smoother, thinner.

The part where the pulse of his heartbeat lies. As I feel that heat, his breath hitches. Such a delicate part—an intricate weaving of vein and sinew—that's hidden, protected, turned in toward the body. But he's offering it up to me, revealing that tender, vulnerable stretch of flesh to my exploration. His breath hitches again, and his head drops, dipping his breath a little closer toward me, closing the gap between us. I want to bring that flesh to my lips, taste it. I cradle his wrist in my hand. Such a large, powerful hand, and he offers it up to me so willingly. Thick hair lies matted on his forearm, but underneath, soft, smooth, heat.

He curls his fingers inward, working his hand around in mine, until we're holding hands. All I can hear is the rushing of my heart as it beats faster, as anticipation breaks through the space between us. My hand is at rest in his, enclosed in its warmth, its strength. Something calm hums in the background of the expectation that mounts as we sit there.

His head moves closer, I can taste the sweetness on his breath. I'm not imagining this. Instinct slides into the driver's seat as I nudge forward until my forehead meets his. Two people in shared silence.

Am I ridiculous for thinking I can find something that looks like solace in this stranger who has swept me off my feet in so few paces? His breathing's thicker, the air between us swollen. I brush my cheek against his, against that thick stubble, and open my lips to exhale fully.

I run my hand up over his chest, to the back of his neck, then up into his hair that's longer than I expected.

He exhales sharply.

My hand slides down to rest on the vertebra where

back meets neck, just under his T-shirt material. Knotted muscle flares out toward his shoulders. His scent intensifies, hotter, muskier, thicker, as I stretch my fingers out and in from that knobbly fusion of bone. Those cords are taut, wound tighter than a spring, as my fingers ride over their waves, then trace toward his throat.

I lay my hand on his chest's plane, his heart's *da-duff* alive under my palm, as alive as the sparks that are sewing the space between us together. Something in him has seen something in me. A rational thought? Not even close, and yet it tumbles through me with all the surety of the tangibly observable.

So long as he's not military.

He lifts my fingertips to his lips, brushing kisses over each one.

I shiver. Where seconds before I stood on solid ground, now I tumble down, down.

There are so many questions that hover on the tip of my tongue. But the sensation of his open mouth on my fingertips is as intimate as shared breath.

He traces over the scar that runs down from my temple.

It's my turn to flinch. How true is the saying that every scar tells a story? This story isn't one he wants to hear. No one does. I pull back from him.

The kisses stop.

As he releases my hand, the roar of the unfulfilled fills me, demanding release, demanding more.

And then he kisses that scar. A soft kiss that speaks with compassion, a recognition from another wounded on life's battleground. "I have to go."

His words gut my soul. How is that possible? This

morning I'd never even met him. This morning, my life had looked different, less than. And now? Now something has taken root and sprouted in me, its roots deep and dark down into my everything.

My mouth is dry as I fumble about for words—the right words—but I come up wanting. Words, which have been so integral to my life, dissolve into meaningless constructs as I bathe in the something that's growing here, in this silence.

He rises from the sofa, his pent-up body moving economically.

As he moves away from me, his presence shrinking, I curse the moments I'll never have again— that last glance as he disappears from view, his departing back as he turns back to look at me, just the simple pleasure of taking him in, all in, with eyes that function, imprinting his walk, his features, his self in my memory. All the things I never considered when…but there's no point in looking backward.

What I have is the richness of his scent that lingers in the apartment, a promise-filled reminder of him that will cling to the walls for hours afterward. His skin, his touch, have left my nerves tingling for more.

His feet barely register on the worn-down carpet that covers our floors. "Skye?"

I turn my head toward his voice.

"Will it be all right if I visit you again?"

I nod. "Yes."

And then his presence shrinks from the apartment, the door closing behind him with a soft click.

Chapter Two

Hours later, I'm still on the couch, replaying and replaying what happened. All of me bristles with something that wants to happen. With potential. The possibility of what could be. For the first time in so long, I have options. Somehow or other, the world has cracked open a door. Have I opened it fully? Or am I still tentatively pushing in fear of what lies behind? Do I even want to step out into the unknown that waits for me?

Chase Rogan.

Heat rises in my cheeks as I kiss my fingertips, echoing his movements. Tiny spasms of guilt and lust spark from the memory. Those same small kisses on my throat, or in the meeting of my collarbone? The back of my neck? The hollow of my stomach? Would he explore that which I'll offer him—will I offer him?—with the same gentleness that he afforded my fingertips? Or is he a greedy man who gulps at nipples and cunts as though devouring was the only possible option?

But…he kissed my scar. That matted, bungled-up clump of dead tissue that protrudes. Ugly. I'd never seen it. I didn't have to. Bumpy, raised, and prominent. What more did anyone else need to know about that hideous mark that divided my life into before and *after*?

I imagine it as purple-red, the angry color of men

whose blood boils over in frustration. The color of rage. On a good day, Ma assures me it's not that bad. On a bad one, she encourages me with the extra-strength foundation, the kind that theatrical people use. To me, the scar's a blot.

But. He kissed my scar. That part of me that runs deep and scared.

Please don't let him be a military man. Maybe he's a man who had a mother who was physically damaged, or a sister, or even a former lover who died tragically? Or he's worked in construction so long he knows the risks of distraction? My thoughts flick back to military. *No.*

A shiver runs through me as I recall his kiss. Soft lips. Hungry lips. Lips that see. Lips that taste. Lips that hear.

I run my hand down over my chest, over the simple long-sleeved shirt I'd chosen that morning, with its modest neckline. Underneath, my bra is built for comfort rather than pleasure. It's plain with no trim and a thin layer of padding to prevent wayward nipples from—what?—hardening, pushing against the fabric, doing what they're designed to do? Mine are rock-hard. Even with that thin 'preventative' layer, my pebbled nipples peek forward. Since *after*, I haven't thought of those nipples. Of the pleasure that's coiled up in their cinnamon-brown tips. Pleasure, as a rule, has not been a feature of *after*.

But those tips haven't forgotten. As for the v between my legs, it's as if all my tension rests in that point, in that hardness concealed by soft folds. Hard and unforgiving, it forces me to feel my body, forces me to confront that I'm a woman whose vitality has slipped somewhere, pushed to the side, ignored. But it waits for me.

It hasn't forgotten that my body wants to feel.

It wants to feel him.

It wants to take him inside of me, pulling him closer, closer, until he melds with me, dissolves inside me, becomes one with me.

Maybe I should have a glass of water and quench the thirst that now burns in my throat? How long have I pretended that thirst doesn't exist? I find my crutches and move through to the kitchen. When will he visit me again? Will he visit me again? Am I being ridiculous? How much of an illusion have I sugar painted in the sky? There's nothing there but hot lust. A need. An itch. A gaping maw of want. That's all.

It's been too long, that's all.

The front door opens and my mother enters. "Skye? Why's the garbage still outside? Didn't you take it out?"

"I did." Her presence is a knot in the air, twisty turning as she inspects and checks for…something. She always finds something. At her silence, I elaborate. "I took it down."

"Then why's it here?"

I recount that morning, skipping over him and all that happened with him. "But I took it down, before I went to get the groceries."

"It's here now."

Ma's already in the kitchen, opening the cupboard close to the kettle, and taking out her glass. Same pattern every evening.

I doubt she even realizes how predictable she is. I wait for the *schlink* sound of the fridge as she opens it, finds her bottle plus the new bottles I bought that morning, and yanks one out. A suction as she eases out the cork, then it's the *glug glug* that scratches down me, causing me to turn away.

I say what's expected: "I'll go see what happened." He might be there. Down by those garbage cans. It's around the back of the apartment block, and the route there goes straight past the super's door. "I definitely took it out this morning."

The second I exit the apartment I can release the breath I'm holding. My mother somehow has a tightrope extending from her in all directions, with me balancing on the wire toward her. I fall off, often. And then she's disappointed. Even if I manage to stay put and somehow fumble my way forward, she's disappointed anyway. Sometimes I want to pull on all those wires and trudge right over to her. It doesn't work that way, though. She is my eyes.

One grasp for the garbage sack and it's pretty clear it's not ours—wrong size, wrong bulge, wrong smell. Garlic and rot intermingle as they reach upward for fresh prey. And it's a few feet from where it's normally dumped. Fucking neighbors, lazy-assed wankers who consider six floors way too many to be bothered with. The neighbor with his fitness habit and his beeping machines that he's strapped to him to record, replay, and reveal his athleticism, can't make six flights down to clean up his mess. So, he dumps it next door and makes it the neighbor's problem. Correction—*my* problem. My mother hasn't taken out the garbage since we arrived here.

I stew. Handling their plastic-covered waste? Hell, no. But if I confront *him*, he'll deny it—how can I tell it's his? It's not like I can *see* it? I can picture his smirk when he says that, and I want to wipe it from him, him and his keep-fit muscles that can't lift a single fucking thing, like garbage. Like I don't know it's him. *Pinche pendejo*—fucking idiot. No, *tonto de mierda*—an idiot of shit. *Capullo* is too good a word. Ah, Spanish, same word for dickhead and flower bud. Go figure.

It took me years to figure out the differences between the Spanish dialects. Italian, too. Now, I can swear across the globe. Small victories.

If I leave that garbage here, Ma will simply come back out here in the morning and bitch at me until it's moved, even with my cast.

Swallowing back the anger that's smoldering like a caged tiger, I reach for my neighbor's garbage bag. I want to hold it at arm's length from me, from possible contamination, but that infernal cast and the accompanying crutches mean that it's up close and cuddly, all his garlic shavings and overripe pineapple.

Before I reach the elevator, the ting-ting noise tells me it's working again. Do I dare risk it, though? My phone's back at the apartment if it cuts out again. The emergency button conked out somewhere around the second elevator breakdown. But head back down all those flights with lazy-ass's shit?

I reach for the button and wait for that *ting* and slide.

The second the doors open, I know he's there. The particular way he takes up space signals to me—*I'm here, I'm here*. I swallow, suddenly nervous.

"Hey, Skye," says Mike, who lives on the floor above and whose voice is lower than most. He's about my age and from the amount of aftershave he's doused himself in, he's out on the hunt. "When's the cast coming off?"

The door clanks shut behind us. "A week or so."

At a push, the elevator can handle maybe four people, if they're more on the lighter end of the weight and height spectrum. It's an old elevator that jiggles from side to side as it shoots downward. Often, you have to remain dead still or the elevator bounces from floor to floor in its own private game of tag.

There's no doubt that the third person in here with me and Mike, is *him*. My heart's already thudding against my chest, every fiber of my being on red hot alert.

Mike shifts from side to side. "Are they going to make you wear one of those moonboot things?"

"I don't think so."

The garlic reek fights with Mike's over-lemon tanginess. It's so sharp it makes my eyes water. And yet, if I turn a little, I can bask in Chase's warmspice, a subtle base note for the louder olfactory punches being swung in this tiny cabin.

"Yeah, when I broke my leg, I had to wear a moonboot, it's way better than those crutches. They can hurt your pits, man, like, so bad."

A hand closes over mine, and I'm relieved of the neighbor's garbage. I don't need to be told that it's him. Mike only believes in helping the parade of women he 'dates' who totter on their heels and who thrum with the hot sterility of a perfume counter. Yeah, the Italians have an expression for how I feel about Mike: *puttaniere*. He's never introduced me to one of his women when we ride the elevator together. What would be the point?

"Is it itching in there? I remember when I did mine, I wanted to get anything down there—*anything*—and scratch it until it bled." Mike's words continue as the elevator finally recoils to a stop.

The doors think for a second or two before half-opening. An arm stretches past me and pushes them full back. Or is he pushing me back?

Mike steps out. "Keep well, Skye. See ya."

That same arm lifts over my head to across my shoulders and gently nudges me forward.

"After you."

His voice resonates calm through me. I clamber out. He's removed my reason for being down here. Really? Isn't he the reason I'm down here?

I should turn back round, head into that elevator, and charge back to where I'm expected to hear about my mother's day at her godforsaken job with those godforsaken people for her godforsaken upkeep of her godforsaken life. "Thank you. For taking…"

"It's no problem." A beat. "You want to get some coffee?"

"Now?"

"Uh-huh."

I want to. I want to. "Here?" How many pairs of eyes will watch me disappear into the super's office?

"TJ's?"

That's the diner on the corner. No less private, but no chance of my mother intruding. "We'll have to make it quick."

"Let me take care of this"—a clank as he raises my neighbor's garbage—"and I'll meet you out front." He pauses. "You're okay to get out front?"

"I know my way to TJ's and back and the grocery

store and back." There's pride in my voice as I say something that makes me echo a five-year-old in content. Small steps but they're mine.

He swishes past me.

I brace as I step toward the unknown that uncurls in my belly with butterfly-shaped wings, ready to take flight. I walk the six paces to the front door but I'm slightly off-kilter. Somewhere between exiting the elevator and agreeing to meet him, I've lost my bearings. My crutches reach for the door that's not there. Fortunately, someone opens it, holding the door for me.

The apartment block's entrance has no steps—thank heaven for small mercies—and opens out onto a busy street. Its roar surprises me every time. Heavy buses chug an infernal bass drum—over humming traffic, blasting radios, and people. People talking on their phones, no, *shouting* on their phones. Piercing, disjointed voices that set the listener on pins and needles all around me as they discuss what's for dinner, why they're late, or how they're losing reception. Footsteps thunder as the ant-like traffic trudges past. I wait for him nearer the wall. Any farther out, and failure to join the stream results in hustle and jostle. Without my cane, I look like any woman on crutches. With the cane, I can feel the parting of the tides on either side. Sometimes someone will call out something like 'cracked sidewalk,' but mostly, folks keep a wide berth. It's as if my condition was somehow catching—a disease that could creep up on them just from being too close.

A few seconds later, he's by my side, that scent an oasis of calm in the rude smog-choked street. We start off together. It's thirteen paces to TJ's. Lucky thirteen? I count them off as regular as a clock ticks its seconds toward each minute.

"Hey, Skye." Angie, one of TJ's regular waitresses, greets me as we enter. "Your usual's free."

"Thanks, Ang." He follows me to the booth in the far corner. I slide in to where the plastic's probably molded to the shape of my butt. I like TJ's. It smells of browning onions, coffee, and frying meat. It's always warm, and they bleach down the counters after every customer so at least I know it's not just cheap and cheerful but clean as well. No missing that bleach burn.

"Your usual? You come here often?" His voice matches the ambience—I'd guess this is his kind of place too.

"They make the best pie this side of the border." Yeah, I'm back with my chirpy-cheep-cheep. Slow and sultry, I am not.

His voice growls. "Best I try some, then."

"I recommend the peach."

"Don't eat fruit."

"What can I get you two?"

Ang's perfume is sickly sweet, a candy apple of scent. She's younger than me, but not by much. Her voice is twangy, and I pick up the lilt in the 'you two'. She's close to the table, closer than normal.

I order. "We'll take some coffee and the pecan pie."

"Great choice." She hovers before sailing off.

I pick up from his last comment. "Don't eat fruit? What? Not at all?"

"Not if I can help it."

"How'd you get your vitamins?"

"Coffee."

I laugh.

He laughs too.

A bolder laugh than I'd expected.

My arms rest on the table. He stretches his hands over to mine, nudging them up against my fingers, before swallowing them whole. My breath hitches. Such a simple gesture that says so much more than I probably should think it does. Still, I'm cocooned in the warmth of that booth with him in front of me, his hands on mine, interlocking with mine, a shared secret.

It's almost like it was before everything happened.

Two mugs clang down in front of us. His hands move away from mine.

Ang's voice is hard. "Here you go."

We wait for her to leave.

"Cream? Sugar?"

I shake my head.

"Same as me. Some say it's too bitter to drink it black, but I prefer it that way."

I sip mine. Time's rolling and my mother will be wondering where I am. "Where'd you come from, Chase?"

"About six floors down from you."

I smile. "That's not what I mean."

"I know what you mean." He sounds upbeat. "I come from a small town, middle of nowhere, out here to help my uncle."

The question that's been gnawing at me has to be asked. I take a leap. "How long you been home from duty?"

There's a long pause as he sips. "How'd you know?"

My heart plummets. "Lucky guess?"

"Helluva lucky guess. Do I sound like the military?"

"Something like that." Shit. Military. *Of course, he's military, of course*. It's my turn to sip.

He dips low, his voice close to me. "You've got the most amazing smile I've ever seen. Lights up your whole face."

So, of course, I smile.

"Yeah, just like that." His hands have found mine again. "Where'd you come from?"

"Six floors above you." I rattle off the answer I give anyone who asks about me. "I work from home, I do translation work when I can get it, I live with my ma, yeah." My *after* story.

"Translation? A language specialist." He makes it sound as if I'd said Nobel Peace Prize winner ten years running. "Which languages?"

"Some Arabic. Spanish, French, Italian—the romance languages."

"From the Latin?"

My turn to be impressed. "Yeah, that's right."

"And who is Skye here?" He lifts his hand to my chest.

All of me is on fire—my body, my soul, my mind; his presence stoking something so dormant in me back to life. He strokes the space between my collarbone and my neck as if it holds something infinitely precious. I close my eyes. Why? They are no longer the windows to my soul.

My voice cracks. "No one, really."

Every touch burns. I want to pull him toward me, pull him so far into me that his flesh melds with mine.

I'm hot and feverish, needing to step outside into the cool air to shake this feeling off. What good can come of this? Of his hands that play with mine as though we've long since been lovers. Men know how to play this game. Me? I'm not so good at it. For all I know, he's eyeing up Ang, and I wouldn't be any the wiser.

But my hands in his hands feel good…right?

He's a military man. *The one thing you promised, that you swore…*

"I doubt that you're no one, Skye."

His words trigger an ache that I've pushed down into my throat that gags me. He doesn't need to know my truth. My body? That he can know.

I muster courage from somewhere. "I'm someone who literally blew my future away. That's who I am. That's all you need to know here." I gesture toward my eyes. "About this."

He doesn't respond, just gathers up my hand and presses it to his lips.

Ang deposits the pie.

I pull back. Somehow, I've forgotten I'm in a diner in the middle of nowhere special, the world unfolding and moving around me. I've closed off the sound and battened myself in him.

He drags the plate across the table. "Let me get that for you."

I used to cringe when I first heard those words. To have to rely on others for so many things? It's not that I'm used to it now—I doubt I'll ever be. The difference is the tone in those words. For some, I'm an awkward reminder of their rude health, their intact senses that they take for granted every waking second of their life. They're the type who want to help me so as to ward off any potential karmic calamity that might change their life in a split-second.

Not him.

I open my lips waiting for the spoon, for the pie, the cream. I touch my top lip with my tongue for a second, aware that his gaze is on my mouth. It's the closest I can get to flirting now that I can no longer bat my eyelashes or look up at him from under my eyebrows. He rests the spoon's tip on my lower lip as if testing its weight. I open farther, and he slides the spoon in. The cream is synthetic, from a can, but the pie is caramelized heaven.

The spoon rests in my mouth as I scoop its contents out with my tongue, before it retreats. I flush with heat as he wipes away a trace of cream at the corner of my mouth.

His voice drops low and husky, "Next time, I'll lick it away."

Lick. I swallow the pie without really chewing. My clit, so long dormant, kicks to life at that word—lick, with all its long ell sounds so like his tongue lapping long and languorous.

"It's good?"

He's talking about the pie, but we both know that's not what he's really asking. I nod, and he repeats the procedure, all the while the word lick, lick, lick, runs through my brain on auto-repeat.

Two more bites in and I push him away. "We can't do this."

"Have coffee? Eat pie?"

He sounds so reasonable, so rational, and on the surface, sure, what's so bad about this? I elaborate. "We can't do this, whatever's happening here."

"Are you married? Engaged? I'm sorry, I forgot to ask, I shouldn't just assume—"

"I'm none of the above. I just can't, all right?"

He withdraws, falls back in his chair. "It's okay, no pressure."

Immediately, the turmoil that's been kept at bay unleashes. Keep him away, yes. No. Don't get involved, yes. No.

I don't owe him an explanation and he doesn't seem to want to ask for one. "I'm not sure how I feel about this."

He reaches for my hand and I don't pull away as he takes it gently. "I don't want to rush you into anything you're not comfortable with."

"Okay."

"Good. Can I get you some more coffee?"

Now I don't know how to answer at all. Isn't this the part where he asks for the check and then ducks with the excuses, the no-hard-feelings speech, etcetera, etcetera? But more coffee?

"I'm all good, thanks."

"Well, you ever want to get some coffee again, you know where to find me."

His voice unbends me. Soft, gentle, kind, all the things that can't be faked. I smile. "Six floors down."

"Six floors down, that's me."

We walk back out into the night that's gathering 'round us. He's close, and occasionally his hand touches my shoulder, my back, with a casual grace that is neither threatening nor manipulative. He's simply a man who's been raised a certain way, to hold open doors, keep to the outside of a street, to guide his woman to safety. Lick, lick, lick. I shake away those thoughts as I've been trying to shake away the deliciousness of his scent—unsuccessfully.

"I've been waiting!" Mrs. Adam's voice carries large and obnoxious down the street toward us. "I said six. And it's now nearly a quarter to seven? Am I supposed to wait here all day?"

"Yes, Mrs. Adams. Be right there," he calls back.

His feet don't speed up; he's still making sure that I can lever myself back toward the apartment block. Of course, I can do it by myself, haven't I been figuring that out for a long while now? Still, it's nice to have someone watch for me. To have *him* watch for me. Not her.

A military man. Anything but a military man—promise that to me. Swear on it.

I swear.

I prattle over the emotions that tumble-turn. "A quarter to? That's later than I thought. It was only the one cup."

He jokes. "Don't forget the pie."

Lick, lick, lick.

We reach the entrance.

He beeps the keypad as he punches in his code.

I grab for his arm. "Wait." For what? I don't know. I do know that I can't leave it here, like this. He turns toward me, and my hands run up over his chest, over his shoulders and up past his neck. I kiss him, without considering anything but here and now. I kiss him, and my body responds to his with a flooding of wetness between my thighs. I kiss him, caring not who sees, what they think, what they could say. I kiss him, feeling the bridge between today and tomorrow crossing to another land, something foreign that's scary, but I can't stop myself from moving forward.

His stubble is rough against my chin and his tongue is anything but leisurely. Intoxicated, dazed, I pull away from my moment's madness.

He whispers in my ear, "Tonight—will you come and see me tonight?"

I kiss him again, drunk on his scent that is stronger, deeper as he wraps me hard and close, and then I seal my own fate. "Yes."

Chapter Three

"Where've you been? I was beginning to think I'd lost you." My mother rests on the couch, not waiting for me by the front door.

"I went to get some coffee."

"Why?"

"Felt like it."

She whines. "You could have let me know."

I could have, it's true. But I'm thirty-five years old, and sometimes I stretch for any kind of freedom without much thought of consequences.

"I was worried about you." She's on the couch, a cigarette smoldering as she watches her soap-of-the-moment. Her words don't direct toward me, they aim and land on the screen. "Are you going to start dinner? I'm starving. Didn't eat a thing all day." She has yet to drag her gaze from the screen to me. She won't. "There's some meat on the counter."

I hustle into the kitchen in part to get started on the dinner that's expected, in part to relive the last few minutes. I kissed him. I reached up and kissed him. And not a chaste kiss but a soul-searching, pulse-raising kiss.

Meet me later? Yes. My fingers tremble as I pick up the meat wrapped in polystyrene and plastic wrap, its watery juices spilling. Red meat. Steak.

The cold meat contrasts with the heat that's slow

burning in my heart, my head, my groin. I take a step back, focus on the steak, remove it from its packaging, and thump at it with a tenderizer, careful to judge the thickness with my fingers before battening one end to death and ignoring the other.

I can still taste him. Taste the coffee, the bitter pecans, the synthetic cream, and him—something sweeter. My chin burns where his stubble brushed me. Is it pink and blotchy? Wasn't that how my mother used to tell I was kissing men I probably shouldn't when I was younger and under her roof? I'm under her roof again, her rules.

I want him to stroke that stubble against the flesh that no one sees. Feel that harsh scraping against my softest, most secret skin. The image causes me to clatter the tenderizer to the floor.

"What's happening in there?"

I call back. "Dropped something."

"Is it broken?"

"No."

"What? I can't hear you?"

"I said, no!"

Her voice is an invasion of the us that is unfolding. *Us?* Okay, the 'thing,' the whatever it is. I switch on the gas and the flame burns hot immediately. Comparisons would be odious. I arrange the steaks in the nonstick pan and wish again that we had a grill that worked.

My heartbeat races upward as if it were responding to some invisible conductor's rhythm. As the steaks start to fry, the fat sizzles, releasing and spitting its juices into the pan, a surrendering to the heat that's changing its molecules, shifting its state.

If—when—I creep down to his apartment tonight, I

won't be the same person afterward. I slap a spatula down on the steak, splaying it into the pan. It hisses back at me, sparking tiny jabs of hot fat on my bare skin that stings.

There will be consequences.

A military man.

I find the cold potatoes left over from the previous night, slice them, and add them to the steaks.

I replay the kiss—the feel of his arms around me, his tongue's wetness, his urgency as he spoke. Each word flips over in my mind. *Will you come and see me tonight? Yes.* The words clutch at my clit, jumpstarting me back to life. Fried steak and potatoes drench my taste buds with anticipation. Would he like steak and potatoes? Would he like to lick, lick, lick?

"What are you doing?"

Ma's in the kitchen with me and I didn't hear her enter at all. So wrapped up in my own thoughts, I'd switched off entirely. Or she's wearing socks.

I twitch guiltily. Me and my military man and our secret.

She's alongside me and the fruity chug of red wine sits heavy on her already. Perhaps it's seeped into her pores, permanently staining her skin, her smell, her taste? Whenever I kiss her goodnight, its alcohol grapey fermentation whispers a trail of poison.

"You've used the wrong pan. Should be the one with the red handle."

I bristle. "It's cooking fine. It hasn't burnt or anything."

"This time." She peers over me. "Aren't you going to add some mushrooms or something? You went to the shops today, right?"

Her presence looms over the pan as though somehow or other it will add to the cooking that's already happened. "Just watch a second," I say, as I go to the fridge to haul out the forgotten mushrooms. Heaven fucking forbid she fetch them out.

"I had such a crap day at work today. Monica—you remember Monica? She still hasn't forwarded me the instructions that I requested ten days ago. How does she expect me to keep tabs on everything if she doesn't send me the instructions when I ask for them?"

She stretches her arm out to stop me, causing me to briefly smack the ball of my thumb against the pan's searing edge. I recoil, the pain stinging.

"Careful, not too many mushrooms at once, they won't brown properly."

I swallow back every word that bubbles upward in my throat, catching and storing them in that net of unsaid that grows larger each day. Sucking gently on the burn that throbs hot, I move out potatoes that smell golden brown to make way for the mushrooms.

"Aren't those going to get cold, now?" She shifts so the counter props her up. Glug. A large swill of wine that she swishes around her mouth before swallowing.

It's a greedy gulp and it makes me want to retreat somewhere else. Ah, but I have nowhere else to go. "They can go in the microwave."

"I see there's a new super in the building. Someone said he's Dickhead's nephew. Can't be worse than him, hey?"

I drop my head so she can't see the flush in my cheeks.

"Apparently, he's some useless wastrel who was fired from the army."

Every word feels like a pistol shot.

"What's worse than a military man? A military man who can't fucking crack it. Pathetic." Glug, glug, glug. "Hope he gets around to fixing that boiler that keeps breaking down. But I won't hold my breath. His type makes more messes than fixes it."

"The army doesn't fire people."

"Dishonorably discharged or whatever. I think that steak's ready now. I don't like mine too well-done."

I flip the steak out, biting back the questions that rattle off in my mind. Dishonorably discharged? Wastrel? Says who? Ma? The neighbors? Mrs. Adams and Cherry Jubilee? Who the fuck cares what they think? I do. They've whispered plenty about me, I've heard the shushings when I pass. They think because I can't see them, I can't hear them too. I can hear them just fine.

She picks up her plate. "You aren't having any?"

"In a minute."

"Maybe a good thing. Looks like you're picking up a few pounds. Just because you can't see what you look like doesn't mean that you can let yourself go."

Any courage I might have about meeting him later, leaches from me, thick and fast. What kind of man is interested in a woman who can't see, who's scarred, who's carrying more weight than she should…and has a cast on?

"I'll take those potatoes from you then, if you don't mind. Krazy Ks are up next, don't want to miss it." She sails past me, carrying her no doubt full plate and her wine tumbler, her sock-clad feet shuffling on the linoleum.

Her absence in the kitchen warms me, the kitchen

clock counting down the time to my heading six floors down, to him. Alone again, I can reconstruct something that feels like self-worth. Patch and piece it together, the way I've learnt with Razia and the survivors' group. *I am kind. I am considerate. I am...lonely.* The word escapes before I can even corral it back. No time for that kind of reminder—not that I needed it. The lock to my heart is so rusted and tight, I doubt the loneliness clamped behind that lock will ever be set free. Still, it rustles on those chains, demanding to be let loose.

I am kind. I am considerate. I haven't been able to look in a mirror for just over two years now. I don't know how my face has changed. Have the years settled in creases around my eyes yet? Have silver strands leapt free from my scalp? Are my eyes glazed over, or can people still see their original hazel? Can *he* still see their original color? A few extra pounds. My body, under my hands that have developed their own sensors, feels as it always has, but no fuller.

There is a chance that the opposite is true, and I've lost a few pounds. It wouldn't be the first time she's lied to me, and it probably wouldn't be the last.

Without that mirror, the visual facts, I can't tell for sure.

"Heading for my bath now." I call out to the TV, the volume of which echoes through the apartment. That means she's at least three quarters of that bottle down.

Inside the bathroom, I curse all the things—the tricks, the sleight of hand—that will remain locked away forever. Makeup, for starters.

I switch on the hot water, pouring in the foam bath that I half-hope will do as it says on the advert and soak away all my worries. No man has seen me naked since *after*. Not a one. Will it be the same?

I strip off my clothes and climb in hastily, so as not to arouse my drunken mother's suspicion. She demands quick shallow bathing. It wastes water, didn't I know. I did, I do. My razor's there, waiting to defuzz my legs. If I remove my pussy hair, she'll know. I won't be able to make sure any telltale signs aren't left lurking around the tub. "What are you doing that for?" she'll ask in that tone of voice that will remind me I daren't even hope for sex, let alone love. Even my most private of acts seem spotlit now.

My facecloth clogged with soap and bubbles, I wash carefully, feeling the rough warmth over my clit. For a second, I relax into the feeling, allowing the heat to rush toward that tight flesh. Will he put his hand there? His tongue? Will he feel me through my panties? Pull them to one side? Or pull them down first? Will he even want to?

His voice, that urgency? Yes, yes, he'll want to.

Will all of that soft hair that curls in the v between my thighs, so unlike the current fashion, repel him? My heart starts its anxious race. I focus back on that cloth, so warm, so rough against my clit.

My nipples are cold and hard as they peek out from the bubbles. Are my breasts as they once were? Or have they slackened a little? I drag the cloth over those pebbled peaks, and sigh at the pleasure they still have the capacity to unleash.

Inside, I am the same person. It's only my capacity to look outside that has changed.

****

It's a quarter to ten. The TV's still blaring. A soft

snoring like a woodcutter with a chainsaw rattles. I know the picture, I remember it well—my mother lies with her mouth open, her neck tilted back, on the couch where she's passed out. She's been like that every night since he died.

Guilt clings to me. *No military men, remember? Yes, Ma, I know. You can trust me.*

I'm dressed in track pants and a hoodie. Nothing to arouse her suspicions.

I lean close to her. "Ma? Ma?"

She stirs. "Yeah?"

I say the words I've said what feels like a million times in the past two years: "Time to go to bed. You've fallen asleep on the couch."

I feel for the tumbler that rests in her hand and take it from her before it spills its contents onto the floor.

"'Kay." She rearranges herself. Then promptly falls back asleep. Her standard pattern is to surface around two in the morning before heading to her bed. Two. That gives me four hours. For all I know, it'll be four minutes and I'm back up here.

Taking my keys from the counter, I wait for the snores to resume. I'm rewarded pretty quickly. With that, I move to the door, unlock it, and slide out into the corridor. The only danger is that Ma wakes up and slides the deadbolt—then I'm screwed.

The corridor at night smells like empty cardboard food boxes, the kind from Chinese takeout.

My heart's in my hands as I maneuver my crutches to the elevator. No one joins me. A slight chill cuts through the air as I climb into that elevator and pray that it doesn't choose now to go on the blink again. I tighten the hoodie under my chin. There's no time for beautiful lace-trimmed panties or satin shaped bras. There's been no reason for it, not after.

He'll have to take me as I am—track-pants wearing, soap tasting, with sensible underwear that's cut from white cotton and has no additional flounces or frills. No makeup and no perfume. I'd brushed my hair and prayed for the best.

Of course, I can't see him as much as I can't see me.

He could be wearing anything, the dreaded socks-and-sandals combo, and I'd be none the wiser. Maybe it's better that way? It's more difficult to hide who you are when you can't stick up a façade. Sometimes I long for the façade. It's safer. Easier. *Safer*.

The elevator opens on the ground floor and I suck in my courage.

Ten paces to the left is the super's door.

I'm nuts, certainly. Who heads down to a complete stranger's door at night, willingly? Me, that's who.

I hesitate before I knock. Conflicting emotions battle for my attention—lust, excitement, nervousness, fear—all twisting and turning. But knock I do. Once, then twice. A second later, I search for the doorbell that's probably fixed on the doorframe. Before I can find it, the door opens and I'm greeted by the warm smell of spice that sets my heartbeat into overdrive.

"You came." His voice is soft and full of promise.

I attempt a joke. "Not yet." And his outtake of breath sounds like a smile.

It's better to crack jokes and plaster over the nerves that are shimmying through me as he steps back and lets me in. I step over the threshold and am sucked in as he closes the door behind me.

"Can I get you anything to drink?"

"No. Thank you."

There should be an awkwardness between us, but there isn't. He lightly strokes my shoulder. "Let me help you there."

And again I let him take the crutches from me before he sweeps me up and carries me to his couch and not the bedroom. Part of me is disappointed, but the other?

My sense of direction is fried, but there's a radio playing from somewhere to the left. Fried onions and meat's strong odor lingers through the room. The couch is low and the faux suede pile is worn down under my hands. A waft of air freshener hits me. Maybe he cleaned a little before I arrived? The notion is quaint and oddly touching. Not like I can see the dust settling. Feel it in my lungs? Sure. I sniff. The air seems clean.

But it's not his place, is it? It's his uncle's. We're both somewhere that doesn't belong to us.

He's at my side, his knees perpendicular to my thighs. He takes my hand, and at once I'm at ease. I ask the burning question: "Is Mrs. Adams expected to live?"

A snort. "Through to the next century at least."

"Her dog's the reason I'm in this cast so I'm not as amiable as I could be toward her." What am I rambling about? His fingers stroke over my hand and under, and I'm reminded how long it's been since I had a man in my life who held my hand for a reason other than to point me in the right direction. Would this man do the same?

"You look beautiful."

Those three words undo me. They shouldn't, but

they do. They unstem a tide of longing that I'd wound up tightly. I want to believe him. Even if it's not true, those words are working their magic. "I do?"

"Uh-huh. You have no idea." His words sound hungry and his lips graze mine.

I clasp his face with my hands. "You shaved."

"I don't want to hurt you."

More words that unravel parts of me. Whenever a man says that, a whole barrelful of pain lies waiting to be uncorked.

"With my beard," he elaborates.

But I think we both know what he meant. "It's fine."

This time when he kisses me, he's patient, methodical, a leisurely stroll about my lips, my tongue—tasting me, licking at me.

It's deep, slow, and delicious. Regardless of what he thinks of his shaven face, stubble still scrapes against me. He sucks at my lower lip, pulling it into his mouth. Then he's back with the slow, long, and deep kissing. It's as if he's making love to my mouth. His hand meanders through my hair, over the back of my neck, and across my face; his turn to imprint the details of my physical body into his skin. Each time his touch slides over that space where my neck meets the top of my spine, my body contracts, my hips pulling upward. How is it possible that so much untapped need sits in such an unlikely knobbly place?

In turn, I run my hand through his dense hair that springs back with each movement. His scent weaves its spell through my senses, and I pull away from his mouth to bury my lips at the base of his neck. Each kiss elicits a hitch in his breathing that I find more arousing than I probably should.

He's wearing a shirt with a collar that's opened up.

I undo the first few buttons so I can slide my hand over his chest, over the tightly sprung hair that nestles there. His skin is hot to touch, feverish almost. If I could melt into him, I would. I work my kisses back up his neck while my fingers stretch over his hot flesh. He groans as I slide his earlobe into my mouth. I know his eyes are closed. For this moment, we are both alone in the darkness, together.

His words whisper something like hope in my ear.

"I don't want to know you here only." His hand lightly touches between my legs. "I want to know you here." He touches my head. "And here." My heart.

Words are only that—sounds made real by breath. His words undo me.

As I continue to suck on his earlobe, he pulls me closer, tighter, his body in my arms. All of me dissolves into this moment, of two people slowly exploring each other, their unspoken language of expression. How difficult it is to tell how a person will show love with their body and yet also, how simple. His lips trace over my neck, marking my flesh while his hands are working slowly over my hips, my waist, as if he's weighing up each bump and curve.

The slow strokes unclasp any fears I may have over his intentions—this man is all lover in the truest sense of the word. In all languages. Lover, *amoureux*, *amante*. Oh, but it's the body that speaks the most eloquently. So difficult to disguise what a body says. It's seldom lost in translation.

By the time his hand slips up under my hoodie, I have lost myself entirely in his caresses that have sculpted and molded my body as if I were something infinitely pleasurable. Maybe I am? Maybe for this man, this body is enough. Although flesh is a feast for the eyes, for the woman, the ecstasy is in the touching, not the viewing.

"May I?" His hand hovers below my bra, firm, possessive on my ribcage.

I grapple to find my voice. Forming words requires a concentration—a thinking—that has slipped away, replaced by feeling. One word escapes. "Please."

"Is that a yes?"

"Yes."

As his fingers trail over my practical bra, I curse the obsession with padding. Under the swathing and swaddling, my nipples push forward, desperate to connect with his travelling fingers that seek out their destination. Fuck those bras with their lack of personality, their lack of sensuality. *Just yank it out of the way*, I want to scream. Or better still, rip the damn thing off. But he's in no hurry. His entire approach is as unhurried as if we have forever this one night. He works up my hoodie and bends his head toward my encased breasts. His teeth graze over the fabric and my hips grind into the couch. What I wouldn't give to watch him doing what he's doing. I run my hands through his hair, working my thumbs back to his earlobes.

When I can bear that gentle grazing no longer, with careful precision he slips the bra straps from my shoulders, slackening my breasts in their cotton prison. Kisses lighter than tumbleweed cover my chest. Each kiss is an awakening.

I no longer remember who I am or where I am, all I

can focus on is the desire swelling in my body, soaking up every kiss, expanding my consciousness, flooding my panties with wetness. A thumb brushes over my nipple that's so hard it almost hurts. I gasp and he repeats the movement. Such a small move and yet, I'm now desperate for his hand to slide between my legs. Softly, he takes my nipple into his mouth and licks. Each lick, each suck, sends shockwaves of pleasure through my body, all gathering in my cunt which would surrender everything I am to have him in me, right now.

But he doesn't move his hand downward. Instead, he works on my other nipple, rolling it between his thumb and forefinger.

My breathing shallows, I'm almost gasping for breath, as the heat spreads up over my body. I grapple to pull him toward me, to undo his belt, feel his hardness.

He releases my nipples before kissing back up my neck.

This time when he kisses my mouth, I wrap my legs around him, pressing his body toward mine. His belt buckle lies against my stomach, its weight comforting, and between my legs, his hardness rocks against me, simulating the act that is to follow.

Am I going to have sex with this stranger who is kissing my lips with such tenderness, whose hand is gently undoing my track-pants, working them open so that he can push his body into mine? Yes.

Impatient, I assist him, yanking my hoodie over my head. The half-released bra unclasps quickly and is abandoned. He's threading each leg back out of my track-pants. All that's left between him and my nakedness covers my cunt that contracts with want.

As he returns to shower my breasts with kisses, I tug at his shirt and pull it upward. His is a chest that works out, with each muscle clearly defined, a ridge, a bump, an ode to masculinity. What I want is something that's secreted deeper inside him. His soul. Would he bare that to me? Would he bare who he is? My own concrete barriers reveal themselves to be nothing more than imaginary constructs. I can't even sense them anymore. But him?

I want you here. His words echo to me.

I undo his belt buckle. My fingers tremble. Will I remember how to do this? The mechanics themselves are straightforward. What isn't, is everything else that's unfolding here.

He wears no underwear, and I encounter heated smoothness under the taut fabric of his jeans.

A moan.

There's a moment's pause as he disentangles from his jeans and his shoes thump to the floor. A cool breeze dusts over me, the space between us wide as he deals with the practicalities of lovemaking, like laced-up shoes, latex condoms, and jeans that bunch at ankles.

Away from his body's heat, my own body grows cold.

"You are so beautiful. So beautiful."

I could get drunk on those words whether they're true or not. Such a simple adjective—beautiful—and yet its utterance has flipped my world around.

I don't gather my hands over my breasts or between my legs to cover myself up. If he sees me through a beautiful lens, then let him look. Let him be eyes enough for both of us.

The mood shifts. He's on top of me, his burning

skin against mine, warming me up, stoking my desire.

He strokes over my skin. I love the roughness of his hands, the grazes and cuts that mark his skin which now mark mine. Would he make me mine? His? A shiver runs through me. Too much hope is never a good thing. But his hand over every dimple, crevice, unrazored hair, warms me up, kindles, if not hope, then a similar cousin to it.

His mouth replaces his hands, light kisses all moving downward, downward, downward.

I part my legs and his breath hitches. I picture his face as he gazes down at the folds between my legs. Can he see the wetness there? I raise my knee. His head fills the space between my legs and his breath on my thighs is hot.

I slacken entirely as he kisses my mound, the soft hair melting under that hot breath. I arch my back toward him, beckoning him closer. Everything I am is concentrated in that nub of flesh, that wishbone-shaped organ. His tongue darts out at my clit and I groan.

He licks again; soft, slow, long strokes.

Pleasure caresses me, dares me to climb its heady peaks. But the soft slowness of his tongue arrests me to this moment. If all the world could retain that deliciousness, there would never be a need to send a man like Chase to war—we would be too busy untolding and delighting in love and its making.

His thumbs work at my thighs, kneading the doughy flesh there. I ache for his thumb to inch forward and lodge in the wetness that's pooling there. I can smell myself, smell how open and ripe I am for this man. As if he can read my mind, his face flattens against my clit, sucking my flesh, that race toward ecstasy kickstarting. I brush my hands over his head, willing him onward yet wanting him to stop. Wait, I want to yell, I don't want it to be over this quickly, this soon.

"Let go." His words are so slight. "This isn't the ending."

With that, his thumb pushes inside me, then his finger, pushing me open, splitting me wide. As he rubs against my walls, his tongue continues its long licking, finding my orgasm and pushing me over.

I pant with release.

My body throbs, my cunt contracting and releasing, squeezing his fingers as his tongue relents.

My eyes are closed. For the first time, I'm glad I can't see him. This moment, when I am surrendered in pleasure, is almost painful. This moment, when the darkness is what I crave most. In the darkness, I am invisible, part of the nothing that is the eternal.

His kisses trail back up toward my mouth. He kisses me deep and slow.

I taste the musky arousal that his tongue, his hands, his intensity, have unleashed in me. It's full-bodied and earthy, a taste that speaks of a self that I barely recognize as my own and yet I suspect it's more me than I realize.

His body presses close against me, its heat burning through me. His hardness rests against my stomach, patient. I want to know his body the way he's getting to know mine. I want to know what he likes, what gets him off, how to make him feel good. But right now, I ache for that hardness to be deep inside me.

Between kisses, I ask the question. "Do you have a condom?"

"Uh-huh." He moves away from me, and the cool rushes in again.

A box opens, a tearing of foil.

I reach for him and he guides my hand over him as we unroll together. A beat of lust drums up. Something so simple, trust. And yet.

My hands steady his hips as he lowers himself toward me.

"You're sure?"

"Yes."

A moment's pause and then he's inside me.

I inhale. A pleasant pain ripples through me. So long, it's been so long.

He starts to move.

I'd forgotten what this felt like. The weight of his body on mine, the crush of pelvises that cannot be deeper, closer, tighter together. The sweat beading on his chest and shimmying across my own. The sound of his breath growing deeper and stronger. And the smell. The rich aroma of two people fucking. I pull him closer and grind him toward me.

That deep in-out motion sends me back toward those pleasures so recently visited. His hands grasp mine and I hang on as he rides me, each stroke of his cock pushing me toward orgasm.

If he were to ask for anything, I'd grant it—my soul, my body, my life, anything. The throb pulses out over me, enveloping me, seducing me with its shuddering waves.

As I climax, my body collapses into submission. I cry out, a shout that breaks my body's long silence for passion.

His cock contracts within me, and his body tenses

as he comes. Locked in each other's embrace, we ride out the waves and I breathe in everything that could be possible. A meeting of bodies, yes, but something else, maybe?

His stillness comforts me. But I tense as I remember what happens next. The rolling off, the contraception disposal, the coldness that replaces the heat with the efficiency of a cement mixer.

I wish I could see his face. I'm glad I can't.

He withdraws from my body and tucks in alongside me, his arm stretched across my chest, his head burrowed in the space between my neck and shoulder. I tilt my head toward his and I kiss his forehead, and then cup his face with my hand.

He takes my hand kisses it. "Will you come to me tomorrow night?"

My heart leaps upward. *Yes.* Reality coldly trickles back in. A military man. My promise. "I'll see."

Chapter Four

I close the apartment door and listen to his footsteps as he heads back toward the steps. My heart's a moth with a broken wing fluttering toward a flame. Down. Steady. Back off. Sex. A physical need. That's what's going on here. Of course, he wants to see me again. I split wide for him, and so soon, too.

Nothing more. Nothing less.

But he walked me back here. Yes, and you're blind if you think there's more to it than that. A good fuck is a good fuck and a great fuck is worth repeating.

A man is a man is a man. Had I not learned anything?

The apartment is like death. Three-in-the-morning still. Mercifully, Ma hadn't slammed the deadbolt closed.

I stumble to my room. My mind's a tilt-a-whirl. I need to shower. I need to rub off his smell that's dripping from me, rub his fingerprints from my skin, his taste from my mouth. My chin burns with stubble rash.

And yet, I want to wallow in his imprint.

I hobble over to my door, easing the crutches over the cheap carpet.

Three short paces.

"Where have you been?"

Was it the noise in my head that woke her? Or the

thumping of my restarted heart?

There's no answer that fits other than the truth. I push my crutches along, hopeful to sidestep a confrontation. Maybe she's half asleep and her question means concern. I crane my ears. Has she turned over and rolled back to sleep?

She emerges from her room to the right, her presence looming forward, all spark and wire and ready.

I brace. Any good vibrations drain away as she closes the space between us, blocking the way to my room.

"Tell me he's not a military man. Tell me that."

There's no doubt she's been up a while, left to marinate and stew in her own righteous anger. Guilt double-barrels at me, a shotgun of paralysis. I swallow and take it. I'm a hostage to my own poor decisions. It shouldn't have been this way. This wasn't how I wanted anything to go. I wanted out. Instead, I handcrafted shackles that won't ever unlock.

"I only want what's best for you—you know that. And I know what's best and it's not one of *them*. Look at what happened to your father." She tugs at my hoodie and theatrically sniffs the air. "What's this one's name? Where'd you even find him?" She pokes my shoulder.

My response is hollow. "I went for a walk."

"Don't give me that. You think I don't know." She sighs. "I hope you're being sensible. The last thing you need is to get pregnant. Blind with a child. You won't even go on disability."

"I make fine with my work."

"But not enough. I should be thinking about my

retirement by now, but I can't even think of that if you go and have a baby. Look at me—I'm up all night, worried sick, wondering where the hell you might be. Once a mother you're always a mother. You can't help that."

"I'm not doing anything wrong."

"We'll talk in the morning." She clicks her tongue. "And stop looking at me like that. You know I can't stand it when you…stare at me like that."

Her parting shot makes me drop my head. Thoughts flick-flack through my mind, the same back-bending motion of should've-would've-could've. I shouldn't have gone to him, she's right. I shouldn't have done many things, and given half the chance, I'd take it all back, do it over, do it differently.

This time I would succeed.

****

The next morning, I wait to hear the door slam behind my mother. I wait a beat of ten before rising to go to the bathroom.

My body sings with the memory of him. I have to wipe it clean. Submerge myself in soapy suds until those memories are sunk through the drains and washed away. My mother's right. He's no different from the others—he's worse.

Chase Rogan, ex-military, current building super, Stranger. An unknown.

Something claws at me, demanding to be heard. *I want to see him. I want to see him now.*

I forego the bath and shower instead, careful to keep my cast out of the water. There is no time for contemplation or consideration. All of me wants to be back with him in that room. His room without

52

boundaries. *There.*

I dress quickly, not bothering to dry myself first, my pants sticking to my skin. Surely this is madness? And yet, I slide into a new T-shirt, find my crutches, and hotfoot to the door. I almost make it to the elevator when I catch his scent in the air.

My body calms, my heart fires up, and all of me tingles with desire.

He stands close and I let out a sigh that's almost inaudible.

"You're up early." His voice in my ear is an invitation. "I've been meaning to have a look at that faulty faucet. Have you got a second now?"

Somewhere a baby cries, a TV blares, and a car's exhaust backfires in the street.

I steady my response. "Time's a bit pressured this morning. But if you can spare a minute?" Is this really me? I sound like bad porn dialogue. And yet, all I want is everything he can give me—in my mouth, my cunt, my ass, all of it.

"Sure, ma'am."

I tremble as I turn back toward the apartment, aware of his every move behind me.

Was it only yesterday that we met? Impossible.

He takes the key from me and opens the door.

I continue the charade. "We had some problems with it again last night. For some reason when—"

The door shuts and his arms are around my waist, pulling me back toward him. He buries his nose in my neck, his stubble grazing the skin there.

I rub my ass into his crotch as his hands slide upward under my shirt to the damp skin of my breasts. I drop the crutches, feeling his solidity around me like a shield to reality.

He lifts me into the kitchen until the counter is level with my waist. And then he strips me down with such speed and agility I buckle with want. His hands shape and squeeze my ass, dipping between them to the sensitive flesh below.

"I can't stop thinking about you."

His words are like cocaine to an addict. I am high, transported by his desire, hovering a thousand million feet above the ground.

He drops to his knees and turns me around to face him; his hands are steady as he parts my legs.

This time, he finds my clitoris and sucks on that swollen flesh as I grip tight the counter. I cry out. A shout. My leg wobbles as I fizz at the greedy sucking of his mouth on me. "Please fuck me. Fuck me." He climbs back up against me, his fully clothed body against my raw nakedness.

"Yes, ma'am."

A condom package tears and I count the seconds before I feel the plunge inside me.

He squeezes my ass again, then slaps.

The sting burns and I gasp. In a voice I barely recognize as my own. "Again."

Another slap, this one harder. And then he enters me hard and fast.

This time, although my body grips him tight inside me, willing me toward my own release, I cannot turn off the fountain of thoughts that his hand on my ass has unstoppered. My skin burns a little, a bee sting, if that. Yet, the action, the violence in it, has me spreading my legs wider, farther. I want him to do it again. No. I want him to bite me. My ass, my breast, my neck. I want him to imprint me with his teeth. I want to bite him. Feel that satisfying clamp onto his body, a temporary owning of his flesh. Push and pinch at the tight taut skin over his muscled arms, his torso, his ass, his thighs. All while he fills me harder, deeper, with that part of him that invades me now.

He cups my breasts, tight, squeezing my nipples as he pounds. His breath in my ear pants, hot, hard, and heavy. His arms threaten to crush me, his embrace is that tight. I am giddy with his lust.

I lean close toward the counter, offering him all of me.

He accepts my silent invitation and his breath quickens.

My own pleasure sinks me into a bliss-filled haze, never quite fully focusing, but a promise of more. Ah, to be so wanted. I wet my lips, reveling in a sensuality that I don't remember as I roll my hips one last time as he slides out of me.

His hand touches that spot on my ass. "Did I hurt you?"

A beat of tenderness.

I shake my head.

"You didn't come." A statement rather than a question.

"Sometimes it happens that way."

He turns me to face him and kisses me. Not the perfunctory kiss of the one-night stand but a soul kiss that lifts the lazy haze of pleasure. With far gentler hands, he lifts me onto the counter, the same counter that I use to prepare every night's dinner, whether I want to or not, and spreads my thighs.

There's a pause and my burgeoning confidence

falters. I move to close my knees.

He stops me, pushes them back. "Let me look."

I rest on my hands, my shoulders slung back. I'm aware of his gaze, can feel that sucking in of space as he gazes at my opening to my innermost me. Something about his voice, his measure, *him*. Somehow, in his presence, I am bold. I toss my hair.

"You are beautiful. Here." His fingers brush against my folds, delicate, reverent.

For the first time, I revel in the fecundity of my womanliness.

He leans closer, his breath on my thighs. "You smell beautiful." A lick of his tongue against my clit. "You taste beautiful."

I quiver with something that looks like hope.

He moves again to my mouth. His kiss is marked with my scent but as his tongue caresses me, I feel as if he's beckoning me into him, that he is marking me, scoring me with his branded tongue. Fire reaches from my clit and races up my spine as I open my body up to him, to his adoration, to his worship.

He takes his time, works his way down my neck, over my breasts, and my stomach. Where once I sought to wriggle away from my own heavy earthly flesh, I now cannot slide into that softness enough. Soft on soft on soft, as he navigates his way around the undulations of my female flesh. I am cast adrift on a sea of sensuality that drenches me with its perfumed spray. By the time his fingers, his tongue, settle onto a steady rhythm on my clit, I am already so close to orgasm that I shudder with bursts of pleasure, a never-ending spiral of delight. I stretch into his casual leisureliness and massage my breasts, occasionally nudging my nipples that are rigid with longing.

I come in waves and waves of holyfuckyeahs.

"That was good." There's a smile in his voice.

What I wouldn't do for a little eye contact, a wink, a drugged-out, dazed, freshly fucked look, anything. Instead, I have to settle for words, those consequential insubstantial things. "Yeah, fuck yeah." I say it slow though, breathy.

He's stroking my face, rounding my chin. It's warm, close, all those things I shouldn't encourage.

"You're one of the nicest things that's happened to me in a long time."

I don't answer him. I was thinking the same thing. But words are words after all. Anyone can say anything when their pants are down and the hormones are settling. A part of me believes him. A part of me *wants* to believe him. "Don't you have to get back to supering?"

"It'll wait a few minutes more."

"Coffee?"

"I'll risk it."

He moves back from me. Best I wipe down the counter with extra strong bleach.

"Here."

I turn toward his voice.

"I mean, sorry, of course…"

I recognize that awkward, the oh-yeah-you-can't-see-me beat.

"Your underwear," he explains.

I reach and take them from him.

"And your T-shirt."

I'm silent for a good long time, the lump in my throat ripping into me, threatening to dislodge tears.

"That was thoughtful."

"You look out for your team."

"Your team?" I raise an eyebrow.

He clears his throat. "Can I help you with the pants?"

"I got it, thanks." From the sounds of his boots on the linoleum, he's turned away—to give me my privacy. I smile. A gentleman. Who knew they still existed? I wriggle the pants back on over my cast. Maybe one day he'll see me in something other than jeans or sweatpants. Did it matter?

I make with the small talk. "You from here originally?"

"Houston, Texas."

So, I was right about the South. I scoop out the coffee that's running low in the tin. "Patriots man?"

"You better believe it."

"And that's all I know about baseball."

He chuckles. "Football. What about you? You local?"

I shake my head. "Nope."

The coffee machine gurgles and gargles as it drips out a reason for him to stay that little bit longer.

"From this little place called Halford, heard of it?"

"Can't say I have."

"Drive by and you'll miss it." I swallow back the memories. "You heading back to Houston once your uncle gets better?"

There's a pause.

I open the cupboard and reach for the coffee mugs. He's behind me, taking them from my hands. His presence behind me comforts. And then he's alongside me, close enough to reach without stretching my hand too much. Maybe he needs the comfort too? What had he seen on his tours? Once seen it can't be unseen.

"That's the plan. Let me get that." He takes the pot from me and pours. There's something about the simplicity, the domesticity of the movement. Him, me, the kitchen, the banality of making coffee. Yet, the recent shared intimacy lingers. It's in the spaces, the gaps, the pauses, whispering between us.

He opens the fridge then closes it again. "You don't take cream, right?"

"Uh-huh." Observant. Military man, remember? As if I could forget. Guys like him are on full alert even when they're miles away from the action. Taking in the little details—like my coffee preference—was part of a normal recon to guys like this. Oh, yes? And who's a guy like this? No idea.

"Are you on leave?"

"No." His voice drops.

Is that wistfulness? Regret? *Bring it back to the chitchat, Skye.* "You got a busy day ahead?"

The spoon clinks against the ceramic as he stirs. The air clams up. He slurps his coffee, sucking it into his mouth with force. If he could glug it, he would.

Maybe I should have asked about something innocuous, something like a TV show or the freaking weather.

He elaborates some. "I don't like to talk about it much. Still gets to me, you know?"

Somehow I know he's not referring to today's busy schedule of fixing broken faucets or attending to errant archaic Maltese poodles.

I scramble about for an answer that's not trite. My body's still fluttering back down to earth, my heart, my soul still airborne. The last thing I'm looking to do is to shutter the connection between us. Connection? Hell, yes.

Another long glug. "I followed my intuition. I was wrong." He steps in the direction of the sink, and the mug hits the metal with a dull thunk. The perfectly okay faucet pumps out water into the mug as he switches it on and rinses the mug clean.

"You don't have to do that. I'll clean it later."

"It's no problem."

He finishes, then walks over to where I'm holding my coffee but not drinking it. I'm digesting his words. *I followed my intuition. I was wrong.*

His hands slide over my arms, holding them firm, close. He rests his lips on my forehead and kisses me. He takes the mug from me, places it down, then kisses my mouth.

Sweet kisses that hum with sugared coffee.

His finger trails over the bundled scar tissue at the side of my head. "We all make mistakes. Sometimes it's difficult to forgive ourselves but we have to. It's the only way to move on."

A rush of shame swills me out from the stomach down. What did he mean? Does he know what happened? Could he tell? A mistake? Mine wasn't a mistake. Had he done the same thing? I start to speak and he stops me with another kiss. A tender kiss that catches my fall, holds me, promises to never let me go. But he will. *We all make mistakes.* Am I making one now, with him? *Forgive ourselves.* Is he talking about him or me?

And I've made another mistake now—there will be consequences. Me and the military man.

As his lips leave mine, the questions mount.

"I'll wait for you, later. Please say you'll see me." This time, his voice is shot through with softness.

And still, despite the whirlwind that's taken root in my mind, I find myself answering, "I'll try."

Chapter Five

A few hours later, I'm lying on my bed, my earphones on, the ambassador yabber-yabbering in French, and I can barely hear her. It's white noise to my anxiety. Mistakes. Isn't life as much about the mistakes I make, as the times I hit the hoop, score the goal, nail the touchdown or whatever. What had he done? What was his mistake? His intuition was wrong? Yeah, you couldn't trust a feeling. Too much like burps of emotion that needed airing.

Yet, warm, cozy, loving-like emotions were unfurling within me. Sure, they were mixed up with grinding lust, but all of the feels were in motion—a cart pushed down a hill either freewheeling to the bottom, or tipping to the side and crashing over? Which would this turn out to be? I picture that upturned cart, push it away.

Imprints of his hands on mine, his cock in me, his lips brushing me, sucking me, stir in my melting pot of fear. Those imprints lull me to let him in. *Mistakes.* He knows what I did. Or can guess. *It wasn't a mistake.* I need to hit the brakes on the freewheeling fast. Or is it too late?

I pause the recording on my laptop.

Focus, Skye, focus. One or two or more of these translation transcriptions and maybe they'd load me up on their preferred supplier list. Maybe. That would mean an end to Ma's money concerns. I could start paying her back. I could maybe find a place of my own to live. Plenty of people who can't see can have their own place, right? They said as much at that guide dog place. I'd get a dog then, too. I'd need to save for Fido as well. Does anyone actually call their dog Fido?

I've unwrapped this particular fantasy a number of times before; me moving out, living somewhere that's mine, resuming the life I once had. Yet, somehow, in the past two years I haven't moved in its direction. I've stayed here. With her.

I've talked it out a few times with the survivors' group. Talked myself out of doing anything about it. Talked instead of done. Easier to talk sometimes.

Fuzzy feelings of hearts and flowers cloud over thoughts of him. Chase Rogan. Strong man, hard man. A trained man built for combat, for violence, for vigilance. *Someone to watch over me*. My cunt contracts.

I'm getting ahead of myself. Two fucks did not a relationship make. Not the kind that would have him and me setting up house somewhere with a service dog out front and maybe a kid's blow-up pool in the back.

I know nothing about this guy. Except that he's a military man. And I know what that means—what it really means.

I start the recording again. It's like a portal into another world—a world where people make decisions that ripple through to people like me. Far removed and yet, here I am transcribing their words. Their meaning is literally in my hands. I do my best to convey what they've said, but what they *mean*, that could be something else entirely. I am devoid of the nonverbal and will be forever.

They say something like ninety percent or more of all communication is in the body. The way we dress, the way we speak, the gestures we make, how close we stand, how much eye contact we engage in—all the things I have to scrabble about to piece together. Now I use fragments of pitch or intonation, varying degrees of body heat and breathing, variations in the energy levels. It took a while to rely on those instincts, the other senses that, contrary to popular belief, didn't automatically make up for my shattered one. At least nothing has developed in these whole twenty-four months. Maybe it still will and I'll be blessed with acute hearing. But I'm still in the dark.

It's said we learn so much through how we take in our information. For me, it was always my eyes. I used to paint, to draw, to sketch—nothing professional, strictly amateur hour—closely taking in my subject, their nuances, the subtle interplay between light and shadow.

That's gone forever now.

All of Chase's gestures point toward warmth, closeness, intimacy. But isn't that the language of sex? It's about sweet nothings, impossible promises, and close proximity. It's about heat and musk and sweat. A letting in, a relaxing of boundaries, a physical closeness that doesn't need sight to exist.

It's about bodies talking, a universal language of magnetism.

Le coup de foudre. A thunderbolt, or love at first sight? Thunderbolts destroy and leave a cindered, smoldering mass. Is that what's unfolding here? In me? Have I been struck down by physical need?

I want to feel normal with him. Like myself. Like the woman I was before.

I force myself to concentrate on the voices speaking through my headphones. This was my future. This. Listening, transcribing, making meaning and sending it out into the world.

My…punishment. My just desserts. My getting-what-I-deserve. I clench down on my teeth. I made this happen. I was master of my destiny, captain of my fate, and I shipwrecked my life. That I have a life raft at all? Lucky. And Ma reminds me of that every single day since.

My fingers fly over the keyboard, stop-starting the recording, interpreting, translating, and typing. The clicking sounds soothe me. It's the sound of normalcy, a get-out-of-jail card. Not for free though—nothing is ever for free.

This is my price to pay.

His words dance in the background. *Please say you'll see me.* I will never see him. An expression that's about as empty as the stock-standard *I'm fine.* When will I see you? Never. Did you see him today? Nope. I felt him, I heard him, I listened to him—what did he mean by 'team'—I inhaled his scent so deeply I reeled from desire, but I sure as shit didn't see him. The more I listen to people's words the more I realize how empty they are, how meaningless. The voices on the recording are negotiating some kind of deal around imports. But neither side is listening to the other's choice of words. Not really. *Please say you'll see me.* Does he want me to see him? See into him? Know him for all that he is? Is that what's he's asking? I know he wants to fuck again. *Please say you'll see me.* The way he said it read more like a plea than a request. A note of fear that the answer might be 'no'. And yet, he didn't wait for my answer. *We all make mistakes.*

That's just it, isn't it? I'm not scared that I'll see him, or scared he'll see me. I'm scared that he already has.

****

The door slams and I stir. One earphone's left hanging and white noise whirs through the other. My laptop slumps against me, open and waiting for instruction. Thank God, it hasn't fallen to the floor—that's an insurance claim I can't make, lack of insurance being the operative factor. I yell, "Ma?"

Her voice fires back. "What are you doing?"

I sit back upright, replace the earphone and settle the laptop into position. "Working."

My bedroom door opens a fraction.

"Are you finished with that?"

"Almost."

She waits by the door.

I answer her silence: "I'll get started on dinner in a second. Just want to finish up this sentence." The sun's rays warm my skin so it's late afternoon, I'd guess. "You're home early?"

"Yeah." She sounds disappointed. A brief thought bubbles up: maybe she wanted to catch me out? "Going to meet up with Estelle later."

"That's nice." Shit. Damn. Fuck.

"Thought we might head out to Ocean Sam's for dinner. After the day I've had, I need the break."

Beat one, two, three, four. I sigh. "Why? What happened?"

She's resting her hand on the door handle now.

I know from the creak of the door and the shifting of her weight. Not that she knows that I can form some sort of picture of how she looks. She remains invested to the limits of her knowledge. An itch starts up on my ankle.

"That asshole Vernon keeps getting on my case. He knows that I know what's going on—he doesn't have to keep at me like I'm some sort of child." She takes a deep breath and huffs it out. "I may have mentioned something like that to him and he might have mentioned something like 'disciplinary.' Fucker. I could do his job with one hand."

I swallow, my world balancing on shifting sands. "I'm sorry to hear that."

"Yeah, well, it's just been a bad day." She stops her rant. "What's going on there? With that ankle?"

"Can't scratch properly with the cast."

"An itch you can't scratch, hey? Sounds familiar."

Bitterness deep-fried in a bad pun. Welcome to my mother.

"Not going to find you scratching about at three a.m. again, am I?"

"Hardly."

She relinquishes the door handle with a clunk. "Don't wait up for me." Her footsteps echo as she retreats. The bathroom door closes behind her.

I remain with my earphones on, work mode appearance switched up to the max. Ocean Sam's about four blocks away. Heart-to-hearts with Estelle last anywhere from two to six hours. There's no way of telling how long she'll be gone. It means I can't see him later. There's too much room for error. She could come back early, or catch me walking where I shouldn't, when I shouldn't.

That I'm a thirty-five-year-old woman, old enough to make her own choices, no matter how bad, is irrelevant. It's as bitter as those plants they tell you not to eat, but I need people now. *Need* them. I will probably always need them.

Chase does not need me to need him.

Perhaps if Chase was a civilian, I would be able to sneak about and play at romance. But he's not.

This morning will have to be enough. It's not.

I can't remember where I was on the recording when I drifted off. I fumble with the buttons to find my place. The shower switches on. My ears prick. She's showering for dinner with Estelle? What's she not saying? Did that disciplinary already happen? Is she out of a job?

Is it wrong that my first thought, selfish and utterly dripping in self-preservation, is that I won't be able to see him if she's here all day every day? Shame engulfs me, threatens to pull me down into its shady depths.

I am not worth it.

A lump catches and holds in my throat. She held me up when I had nothing to hang on to.

The shower shuts off.

I listen to her padding through to her bedroom, the clacking of hangers as she chooses something to wear, the pacing back and forth from the mirror to the cupboard. I doubt she's seeing Estelle.

A little while later, a perfume cloud, sickly sweet and cloying, drenches me. A tumble-turn of dread flips in my stomach. Who's she seeing? Is it a date? Why is she lying?

I jump as she calls out to me. "Skye, don't latch the

door." And then she's gone.

A crumb trail of aromas assails me as I hop into the passage—the perfume, her cherry blossom body lotion, hairspray, and cigarette smoke.

I slip into her bedroom and make my way over to the vanity that sits opposite the bed. My fingers trail over opened cosmetics, a powder puff squeaky with talc, eyeliners with worn-down ends. It's how it used to be when I was a girl. All the secrets of womanhood used to beckon from that vanity. My mother would color in the cracks. Her beautiful face would emerge as something less broken, filled in. I would be alight with awe.

It's still a mystery to me, these womanly secrets that encompass so much of what we're told femininity is. I pick at my jeans and T-shirt. There are no frills or bows, or soft scooped edges. My face is bare, without enhancement. No jewels at my wrist or throat or ear lobes. No bathing in perfume.

Does he find me womanly? Feminine?

A lipstick tube lies on its side. I slip off the lid, wind up the stick and inhale its fruity slickness. My mother's coloring is my opposite. Where she is blonde, fair-skinned, and bright blue-eyed, I am dark, olive-toned, and brown. I press the lipstick to my lower lip and smear its magic. It is glossy or matte? Am I in the lines? My mother's shaped the stick where she's gripped the wax between her lips, causing a pinched edge. Without the rounded tip, I improvise a cupid's bow.

The lipstick feels soft and slidy, a little cheap in formulation. I rub in the product with my finger. She used to wear pillbox red. Does she still? Or has she switched out to something pinker or earthier even? Those details draw blanks. My image of her is frozen at two years ago. Her hair fell to her shoulders in bleached waves with pepper gray roots. She'd curl the top sections by sleeping in pin curls. Not for her the curling iron or heated rollers. Does she still do that? Maybe it would amuse her to know that to one person she will never age further than fifty-seven. No more wrinkles added, no more sagging jawline or slackening belly.

As I sit here now, I slide her features back to when she was younger, in her early forties, when Dad was still with us. She smiled more then. I don't think she smiles much now. I can hear it in her voice.

I replace the lid on the lipstick and feel around for a cotton pad or tissue. The wonders before me are even more a mystery to me now—even further out of my reach. Red-stained lips never suited me anyway. I wipe the color away.

Who has my mother gone to see, her face made up, her body doused in scent? I push away the whisperings that started up the second she switched that shower faucet on. For a second, my stomach lurches as I imagine her with him. Was he that kind of man? A man free and easy with his affections, a lover of many and yet a lover of none? Was she six floors down, in the super's room, reveling in his heat?

I scrunch the tissue in my hand.

He's not like that. *Isn't he?* How would I know? Maybe it's because I'm not feminine, not girly. A novelty.

I fumble for one of her scents. It's old-fashioned, rich and heavy with spice. I spray it into the air, letting the droplets fall onto me.

If she's out with someone tonight, someone male, she won't be early. *Don't wait up*, she'd said.

****

His kiss is a relief. I exhale against his cheek.

"Are you all right?"

I press closer to him. Was it that she wasn't here when I arrived? Was it the haste with which he pulled me into his arms? Or was it simply the comfort of his chest against mine? "I'm better now." Which is the truth. Close to him, everything else is silent. My thoughts, the outside world, my doubts, my fears, *everything.*

"I got you something."

My heart starts to pick up the pace. "You did?"

The pride in his voice is unmistakable. "Can't have you climbing up and down these stairs every time the elevator busts." He presses a key into my hand. "It's for the service elevator."

I frown. "I don't understand."

"It's for the service elevator 'round the back of the building. I'll show you."

"Isn't that for…emergencies?"

"And big-ass deliveries and people moving their furniture in and out. And now for you."

Mixed emotions twist and turn. "But you have to put in a request…" I leave the key on my outstretched palm.

He folds my fingers over then presses my hand to my chest. "No, you don't. I have the authority to approve it. Request granted."

My first thought is *yay, no more having to slog my way up those shitty stairs*. But right behind it is, *it's not like flowers or chocolate or a date with dinner and fancy wine.* And, bringing up the rear is, *why*? "Why are you doing this for me?"

He races his fingers through my hair. "No reason."

He kisses me again, this time slower, softer.

I press. "What if someone finds out? Won't someone notice me using it, ask how come and put in a complaint? I can't have something go wrong here, you know. Thank you, but I can't accept it. It wouldn't be fair." I hold up the key.

"Is it right that you use the stairs?"

"It's just the cast. It'll come off and then everything will be back to normal."

He hesitates, but he says the words nonetheless. "But you're…you'll still be—"

"Blind? Sightless? Visually impaired? I know what I am. I also know how to climb those stairs. Each flight has twelve stairs, three paces at each landing. And, get this, each flight has a handrail. It's this amazing invention that lets me rest my hand so I don't fall or trip, which to come to think of it, even when I was sighted, I still did. Tripping up my own feet was a big feature back then, and it's less so now, thanks to this. Maybe I should thank myself more often—I can now do stairs, just fine and dandy." I turn my hand and let the key drop to the floor. "Don't do me any favors. I don't want them, I didn't ask for them, and I definitely don't deserve them. Give the key to one of the older people in the building, starting with Mrs. Adams. She'd love to bypass the entire public elevator thing."

"I didn't mean to insult you."

"Forget it." Tension prickles under my skin. It's a thousand sparks of high voltage crackling and clicking for a charge. My swollen ankle throbs with indignation.

"What's more pathetic than a blind woman? A blind woman who broke her fucking ankle tripping over some bitch's dog, that's what. Now, I'm doubly disabled." I air quote for added emphasis. Angry tears threaten to spill over my cheeks, which fuels a gut punch of shame. "At least the cast comes off. Then maybe you won't feel so sorry for me." He reaches for me and I shrug him off.

"It's not like that. I wanted to help you."

"I didn't ask for your help. I don't need it. I don't need anyone's help."

As I fumble to point my crutches back in his door's direction, I'm overwhelmed with a self-loathing far more crippling than a blown-out optic nerve or a broken bone. "Is that all I am to you? A pity fuck? Is this your idea of giving back to the community?" I mimic his voice. "Hello there, little lady, you look kinda crippled and pathetic, but I sure wouldn't mind boning you a little, how about it? Make you feel better in the morning. Whaddaya say?"

Pain lodges in my throat as I choke back the tears. I don't even know if he's still in the room with me, I'm so lost in my own downward spiral. All I'm aware of is the world above closing up on me, the space for air growing smaller, smaller, smaller still.

I lurch forward with the crutches, my bearings scrambled. His hand—soft, gentle—guides me in the right direction. The simple gesture is both unexpected and undoing. I crumble. My head hangs downward as I sob. My body convulses as it rides the waves of emotion.

It's a while before he stretches his hand across my back and strokes my neck, my back, my shoulders. He doesn't whisper or say anything, only that soothing, repetitive motion.

I wipe my eyes with the back of my hand. I open my mouth to say something but every word is corralled back. This is me. This is who I am. An unholy mess of self-recrimination. Anything I say cannot change that.

"You want some water?"

I nod.

He leads me to his couch, seats me, then heads to the kitchen.

I sniff and snort with neither grace nor charm. The water is cool and filtered. I suck it up.

He sits next to me, close, his knee touching mine.

Another small intimacy. I am still here. He is still here.

My voice is unsteady. "You didn't shout at me."

His hand finds my back and resumes its steady stroking. "You're hurting. No use making something worse."

The silence unnerves me. I grasp at something, anything, to steady me. "What did you mean by team? You said that you always look out for your team."

"My unit. My men. We work together strong as a unit. Always prepared. Always looking out for each other."

I finish the water.

He gently takes the glass from me. "Sometimes the only thing you have out there is your guys. It's a long way from any kind of home."

There's that wistfulness in his words again. "Did you always want to be in the military?"

His voice resonates. "There's no greater honor than to be able to fight for your country. I always believed that."

"Do you still?"

There's a silence. "Nothing changes what happened. But it doesn't mean I don't believe in what we're doing out there."

I remember his description—mistakes, he called them.

"What was your rank?"

"Unit leader, Special Forces." The pride bursts in his voice, and he moves his chest forward as he speaks.

A mental picture illuminates with that knowledge.

"Not your regular soldier, then?"

He chuckles. "Nope. It's better."

I shudder at the thought. A regular soldier winds up as dead as those in Special Forces. Both are returned home in body bags and given a heroes' send-off. Both have to scrabble about to forge a living out of the military once they leave. Was Chase the same? Is that why he was here? "Bet you've probably run into some humdingers."

The slight motion in his body suggests he's nodding but he doesn't qualify. "They train us up real good. Always prepared, like the Boy Scouts. You never know what the enemy can or will do in any given situation, but you've trained the crap out of the possibilities."

"With live guns and things?"

His turn to be full of the snap, crackle, and pop of emotion. It ricochets off him like those bullets he no doubt triggered. "Yeah, with live ammo. Gotta be on your game. When you're in it, it's just you and the enemy. You or him. And if it's a hostage situation or similar, you've gotta make sure you take out your target immediately. Neutralize him."

I go completely still at that. He's dancing too close to parts of my past.

He's almost apologetic: "I guess it's not for everyone."

"My dad served."

"He did?"

I direct the conversation elsewhere. "You ever get a predator situation? And have to prevent an extra-terrestrial invisible hostile from tearing apart your platoon?"

"And she speaks action films, who'da known?" He sighs, locking his fingers in mine. "Off the record?"

"Uh-huh?"

"We managed to contain the situation, but the alien got out."

"It did?"

"Yeah. Got a lotta flak for that one from the boys upstairs. Said we got sloppy. I think it was the dog that did it. Too distracting."

My tears have long since dried, my prickliness dislodged by the strange comfort of this near stranger.

He pokes his finger into the sensitive spot under my arm. "You won't tell anyone about that, will ya?"

I yelp.

"Hey? Hey?"

He repeats the jabbing, fast discovering my ticklish spots that have me jumping about like a freshly caught fish. I cry out. "Peace, peace. Mercy, have mercy."

"Who is this mercy?" He relentlessly continues. "You want me to stop?"

"Yes. No. Yes." His fingers squirm and wriggle down my sides, and the pleasure-pain principle stretches to its limits. "Get off, military man."

"That's sir to you, civilian."

Another jiggle and wriggle to my ribs that makes me slide off the couch, my cast pinning me to the site of the attack. "Off, sir." My words intersperse with laughter, the kind that causes fresh waterworks. My sides ache with laughter as his hands finally let up.

He pulls me back onto the seat and readjusts my T-shirt until it's straight and respectable once more. "Hey, young lady, don't you know it's bad form to mess with a Special Forces guy? We've got skills, you know."

"Oh, yeah?"

"Um-hum."

His hand slides up my leg, closer, closer, closer to my cunt. "This is what they teach you?" His body warms mine as he closes the gap between us.

"They do. And some of us are very, very good at it."

"Did you get a medal?"

"Honey, you better believe it." He unzips my jeans and peels back the top of my underwear, softly kissing my belly.

I arch toward him. Under my hands, his muscles are taut, hot. All of me relaxes into the couch as he spreads my legs and slides my jeans, my panties, off.

"You have no idea how beautiful you are."

That much at least is true—I have *no* idea.

He kisses my mouth, a tender sweet kiss that speaks more of something other than lust.

I dismiss that thought—Chase does not need my need. I unbuckle his belt and release his erection as he kisses me. His penis hardens further as I draw my thumb behind its head.

A slow moan from him.

His kisses trail down my neck, while I grip his hardness and slowly work it in my hand.

His breathing lengthens, holds.

I continue my exploration, and cup each ball, rolling it softly, feeling their weight. He's lost in the motion of my hands, and my own arousal mounts. How can any woman, or any man, for that matter, not delight in the giving of pleasure, the sharing of themselves with another? I kiss him, sliding my tongue in and out of his mouth, capturing his lower lip and sucking.

"I want to be inside you."

My cunt contracts.

He hands me a condom.

I open the packet and smooth it down over him, his hardness thick and ready in my hand.

Chase eases inside me.

I'm once more struck at the beauty of his filling me. For a moment, we lay like that, with him inside me, his weight resting lightly on me.

"I want to fuck you." Those are my words to him. Fuck. Guttural. Dirty. Devoid of tenderness. He flips me around so that I'm astride him, his back against the couch, my knees pushing into the worn cushioning. Has he any idea how good he feels? I grind against him in a circular motion, my hips rotating.

He groans.

I ride him slowly. Deep, measured strokes that swell my clit. From here, I am master and commander of my own sexual destiny. And yet, unspoken, a thread runs between the two of us, connecting us, uniting us. It's his acquiescence that has given me power. With each hip thrust, I forge that connection further.

"That feels amazing." His hands grip my hips but don't push or pull.

I take his hands and guide them upward onto my breasts, onto my hard nipples that ache with sensitivity. He squeezes them gently, his thumbs brushing over that sensitivity that flames the fire in my clit. If only we could stay together like this, the bliss—the untold, heavenly bliss—of our coupling. No. Fucking. As I hear the words in my head, a current surges through me, through to him and we move together toward the orgasm that circles me.

There's no hurry, no need to grunt or grasp, just a slow inexorable sailing toward the inevitable. The orgasm builds in my clit, my cunt, my anus, throbbing, pulsing, building, higher, further, greater, more. I hold on as it peaks, reaching, reaching, reaching for more. And then it breaks and I ride the waves that contract and relax through me. My mind blanks. It's only pleasure. Only joy. Only love. A magical ride through the cosmos, the stars, the alpha, the omega, the everything.

Inside me, he tightens, his shaft pulling up from his balls and stiffening for one last release. Our bodies push together as his orgasm meets mine.

A thin film of sweat rests on his chest as I reach down to him, find his mouth, and kiss him.

He grasps my head, passion alive in the braille of his fingertips.

How many seconds, minutes, months have passed by in the length of that kiss? He still rests inside me, neither of us ready to break the spell.

Our lips part, and our foreheads connect. He breathes me in and out, and I breathe in him. I trace my finger over his lips, lips that are smiling, that meet in butterfly kisses over my fingers, my hand.

"We came together that time."

"Did we?"

"Uh-huh." He turns my hand, kissing it over and over. "I've never had that happen before."

"Me neither." I find the end of the condom and lift myself upward so that he slips out of my body. Everything that felt swollen, urgent, and vast now seems so small. So vulnerable.

We sit on the couch together, separate, each in our disheveled disarray. I scramble for my panties, my jeans, and pull them back on as if to hide the memory of what just happened.

It meant nothing. Two lonely people. Probably the saddest and most familiar story of all.

"Let me just take care of this." He gets up. He means the condom and its disposal. The cleaning up afterward.

The physical part is always the easiest. A quick wash and it's over with. But anything else? Is there anything else? *You know there is.*

"I have to go. My mother will be home soon. She'll be expecting me."

"You don't want to stay for a drink? Maybe watch something?"

I bristle. "Really? Watch something?"

"You know what I mean."

"Yeah. I know."

I hurl myself up onto my crutches. "Thanks for the water."

Chapter Six

The next morning, my head pounds—the inevitable aftermath of tears.

My mother smacks and bangs around the kitchen. Saturday morning.

I stumble out of bed, have a pee, then make for the inevitable reckoning.

Fresh coffee brews and the TV is already on, switched to some reality show about young couples buying up huge fixer-uppers.

"Who the hell has money to afford something like that at that age?" My mother's voice pulsates with bitterness. "Four-bedroom house, basement, all-new wood floors, great area—suburbs—close to the schools, huge yard, just needs a breakthrough for the open plan experience."

"Maybe they've been saving."

She makes a grunting sound.

"Do you think one day, a generation or two from now, they'll build all the walls back up? Ask, why the hell is the kitchen in the living room?"

Her cigarette smoke burns my nostrils. From the dense fug, she's been up a while, and I'd bet that's coffee pot two or three.

"We're going to have to talk…about things." She inhales deeply. "Turns out there's no disciplinary."

I wait for her to fill in the blanks.

"I'm out."

"Out?" A hook sinks down my stomach, catching my insides and pulling my throat with it for good measure.

"No more job. Fuck him. I was going to quit anyway."

"What happened?" I piece together last night's shower, the meeting, the perfume, all of it building a picture that I don't want to see. "I'm so sorry."

Another grunt.

There's a knock at our door.

I turn toward it. "Who's that?"

My mother pushes past me. "That jerk of a super. Fucking faucet's acting up again."

"Genuinely?"

A million different responses rush through me—retreat to my bedroom, disappear in front of the TV, hide in the shower—but I don't do any of these. I can hear his voice doing the whole *hey, how are you* thing. Shit, they're even mentioning the weather. Within seconds, he's behind me in the kitchen.

"Morning."

I tilt my head in his direction. "Hey!" Nothing to see here, folks.

"What seems to be the problem, ma'am?"

Something hard and heavy clanks down on the work counter. I'm guessing a toolbox. My throat dries entirely.

"Look here, when I shut it off, watch." My mother's voice shrills as she explains about the fucking faucet that's acting up again.

I talk over them. "You want some coffee?"

There's acid in her voice. "Let the man do his

work, Skye."

I can feel the love from here.

"Think you can fix it properly this time? I don't see why I should call out a plumber when you're supposed to be fixing it. Think you can do that?"

"Yes, ma'am."

This time? Had he been here before, then?

My mother's lighter clicks and flicks before a smoke trail breezes past me.

I busy myself making a breakfast I don't want. In the background, Joe and Sarah have just fetched the keys to their new starter home, isn't that great? His presence unnerves me. I must have colored up at the sight of him. Did she notice? Is she watching me now?

I take down a bowl, fill it with bran cereal, careful not to walk close to him as I head for the fridge. He's swallowing up that counter—oh, the things we'd done just yesterday on that counter. Is he remembering that, too? I drop my head, busy in the art of looking busy.

"Tell me…"

My blood runs a few degrees cooler at my mother's inquiring tone.

"What's it like to know you let your country down? Thousands of men give up their lives fighting for our right to drink coffee in a free nation."

I nearly drop my bowl. "Ma—"

There's a long pause in which my mother's venom works its way under the skin. Let the country down?

"Ma'am, I assure you, no one is more ashamed than me at my conduct. It's something I live with every day."

She makes a clicking noise with her tongue. "When I think of my husband and what he did, and how you're here with your tattoos and your long hair, disrespecting the flag."

The shuffling clunk at the worktop ceases.

"Ma, what are you talking about? Leave him alone."

She turns on me, spitting and biting. "Your father lies six feet under. And what did he get for his service? Nothing. That's what. And deserters like this one, they get to carry on like nothing ever happened."

Deserter?

His voice is firm. "Ma'am, I'm no deserter." The faucet turns on, the water rushing as it hits the sink. "All finished." He turns the faucet back off.

A loud slap as his toolbox closes. "I'll let myself out." He brushes past me, everything about him tense and coiled.

Reach out, follow him, something. My frustration roots me to the spot. "What the hell, Ma? What in the actual hell?"

The front door slams shut.

"I can't stand to see him waltzing around here. When I think of all that your father went through—"

"That's not Chase's fault."

"It's Chase now, is it?" A beat. "Oh, how stupid am I? He's the one you've been *busy* with, right? A yellow-bellied, good-for-nothing deserter. Wow, have you chosen well." Sarcasm blends together with the poison into her own personal brand of Molotov cocktail.

"You're clutching at straws. He's not a deserter."

She laughs. "What else do you call someone who was dishonorably discharged?" She puffs her smoke into my face. "Those traitors aren't fit to lick our boots.

Your father would—"

"Not judge a man without the facts?"

"I've got the facts all right, and that man's nothing but a lowlife."

"Have you spoken with him? Or with Mrs. Adams? Or with that jerk who keeps heading up the building committee?"

"Why don't you tell me how you really feel?" Her tone reeks cool, calm, and collected.

Shit, I hate her when she's like this. Hate her. She knows she's got me by the short and curlies, and she's not going to let go. And damn it if I haven't let her tighten her grip. "Maybe that's a good idea?"

"'Scuse me?"

"I said, maybe that's a —"

"I heard you all right. You don't know how much I have to bite on my tongue around you. Make sure I say the right thing, don't want to trigger you off. No more little episodes. You know how difficult it is to see your own daughter—your own daughter—with a bullet wound in her head? Do you? You have no idea. None. You didn't think of anyone else but yourself. You always think of yourself."

I can no longer feel the dig of the crutches in my armpits. I'm numb all over. The more my mother talks, the more I drown the sound out, let it wash over me.

"I've done so much, so much, and there you were, lying in a hospital bed. And when that doctor said that you'd shot out your optic nerve, I didn't know what to do. Why me? Why my daughter? It was so difficult for me. And your father wasn't here. He was never bloody here and when I needed him the most, he wasn't fucking here. Is this what my life is? A dead husband

and a daughter who tried to kill herself? What did I do wrong? What could I have done that was so wrong to end up like this?" Her tone's cracked. Deep wracking sobs hurl through her.

I hate that sound. I know I'm supposed to go over to her, comfort her, but I can't. I can't physically move forward. Tentacles of need have wound their way up from my feet, encircling my entire body. I can't breathe. I can't think. I'm paralyzed in their grip.

My words are robotic, monotone, automatic. "I'm sorry, Ma. I'm really sorry."

She's sobbing and coughing. Somehow, through it, she lights another cigarette. "Why did you do that to me? Why? Why? I don't understand why you'd do that to me? To me, your mother?"

"I didn't do it to you." I marinate in her secondhand smoke. "I did it to me."

But she's not listening. "How can you not think of what it would be like for me? You're my daughter."

"I'm sorry, Ma, I'm really sorry."

The sobs subside.

I reach over to her and pat her shoulder. Her body half-turns toward me, her tears dampening my T-shirt's shoulder. She smells like my mother, Jade. Like the woman who gave birth to me. But even with digging deep, I can't unearth any empathy—that numbness weakens my capacity for anything. For that alone, I am trick-tracked by pity, but not empathy.

She reaches over my head and strokes. "I do love you, my girl."

"I love you, too."

We part. She fumbles with the coffee pot. Normal life programming resumed. "I hope you're not going to carry on seeing that man."

"I'm not seeing him." The lie trips out.

"You made me a promise."

I swallow. "I've nothing to do with him. Nothing."

"Because if I find out you're with him…you swore. No repeating the past. No men who love their country, not their women. You promised."

"I did promise."

"And that scumbag…he's not worth it." Her tone slices me. "He doesn't know what it takes to handle someone with…needs. Traitors like that bail at the first taste of difficulty. Your father used to tell me about men like him."

I make a noise that sounds like assent. Somehow, I suspect he can do better than me. Better than the reception he received here, at least. Better than the drama, the histrionics that punctuate life here, with me, in this cramped apartment.

She's right—Chase does not need my need. The numbness uncoils slowly.

"You better get dressed. Aren't you going to your meeting?"

My mother's voice is alien. Meeting?

"The group?"

The depression-and-sadness group—Razia and the survivor's group. "Sure. I'm heading out now." I click-clack my way back through to my bedroom. How many of these meetings have I missed? Since starting? None. Every Saturday, I'm there, usually first to show. The only place I can relax and unfold. That's not true. Not the *only* place.

I shower, dress, and fetch my purse. As I emerge, I sense she's left. The apartment seems freer, lighter.

"Ma? Ma, are you still here?"

No response. Nice of her to let me know. What, like the other two million or so times she's done this? What did Einstein say about hope vs reality?

The ding-ding-ding sound signals the elevator's current state of disrepair. Shit. I remember that key I tossed back at Chase. Remember then the heat that we generated. I swallow back the memory. Six flights of stairs in a downward capacity.

I reach the top of the stairs, rest on the bannister, then swing my crutches widthwise under my arm. I visualize him coming up to meet me. What kind of tattoos does he have? Does he have one of those ones that start at the navel and then beckon the viewer closer? Or does he have a dragon stretching out across his shoulders? I imagine him lifting me over those shoulders again, carrying me to his bed, and throwing me down, poised above me as he ekes out my patience before pounding me into submission. My foot falters and I trip down a few stairs. Shit. My heart's racing now, but no longer from lust.

Reality is in that apartment. Reality is right here right now with no help, just me, negotiating in a world that doesn't see me as much I can't see them.

He doesn't meet me in the stairwell.

I get to the bottom, my adrenaline racing for a moveable finish line.

Any chance of being on time for my meeting vanished with that ding-ding-ding. I can't help myself. I head to his door. I raise my hand to knock but stop short of following through. No, the meeting, that's important, that's the future.

I half-hope he finds me at the front door, in the

corridor, outside the building. But he doesn't.

Saturday morning rolls out as it has before. I sit at my meeting, my coffee in hand, listening to my fellow survivors, a word that sizzles me in shame. I am no survivor. When it's my turn to share, I edit my week. Has it only been a week? I'm dying to talk about him. I feel his name unbidden on my lips, springing into spaces, calling forth. I stop myself. He is the super's nephew. And we fuck.

I can't stay with my mother.

I don't mention the fight with her. There's no time to head into the ins and outs. Or rather there is, but I want the meeting to be over with.

"Skye?" Razia, our group leader tries to get me to expound. "Any progress as yet on your plans?"

"I checked out one or two apartments. The rent was prohibitive."

"And the work? Are you finding that you're gaining some independence with your translation?"

"Yes." I hesitate. "It's starting to come together."

"Do you want to talk about how you feel about living on your own again?"

Everything wells up in me, ready to purge. "Not today."

The meeting moves on and I zone out. Today, I don't have the strength to confront my demons who I'm so familiar with I should give them pet names. They hunker behind every move I make.

The meeting wraps. I ask the cab driver to drop me at TJ's on my way back home. Angie comes over in seconds.

"Hey, Skye, dish up all the deets on that one. Shit, I could eat him up with my eyes." She giggles. "Where'd you find that lunk of a hunk?"

"You know, the usual, hanging about on a street corner."

She thwacks me with what I suppose is a menu. "You're terrible. What's his name? What's he do? He looks like he works out a lot."

"He helps invalids up and down the stairs. That might account for his superior strength."

A pause. Then she roars with laughter. "Yeah. So, the usual? Coming right—"

"No. I'll have a strawberry milkshake. Can you add extra marshmallows?"

"What? No coffee? The machine'll protest."

"Let it."

Around me, a woman herds her three small kids into a booth.

One whines: "My chocolate's melting."

"Why haven't you eaten it yet, honey?"

"I wanted to share it with Roy and Dee."

The mother stops a second. "Isn't that the sweetest reason." Her entire tone speaks of exhaustion and quiet love.

Angie brings my milkshake. "Extra marshmallows."

The glass is tall, wet, cold, the smell of synthetic strawberry subtle under the pow-wow of coffee. I take a sip, the pink strawberry sweetness fills my mouth, a sticky link between childhood and present day.

"Looks good."

His voice flips my stomach.

"May I?" He pulls up a chair next to me.

Before he has a chance to speak, I ramble. "Anytime my father was home, he'd take me out every

Saturday morning for waffles and milkshakes. We'd go running 'round the park and on the way back we'd stop into his favorite diner, M&B's. It's been a while since I had one of these." I push the glass toward him. "Would you like to try?"

He takes it from me, his hand brushing mine.

With that gesture, I release tension that's been gathered since this morning. I'm not my mother, no matter how much she likes to bleed through those identity boundaries.

"Maybe it's a little sweet for me." He pushes it back, takes my hand and brings it to his lips. His voice drops. "He must have meant a lot to you."

A lump wedges into my throat. "He was my world."

He kisses my hand again.

I push aside the memories of my father. "My mother—"

"You don't have to explain. She's only acting on the intelligence she's gathered. It's not accurate, but rumor mills seldom are." Frustration laces through his words.

"She was rude."

"More like ill-informed. I'm no deserter. Wouldn't be sitting here before you if I were. She seemed upset, though. Sounds like your father was her world, too."

I scoff. "Hardly. They fought all the time. And the way she carried on—" I stop short. I draw long and hard on my straw, sucking up my strawberry past.

He leans forward so that only I can hear him. "I'm no deserter. Only thing I ever wanted to be, growing up, was in the military."

A longing grips his words, something I recognize

in my own lust for a past that I can never have back.

He relaxes back into his chair. "Every night, I dreamed of wearing the uniform, being called up for duty and doing my country proud. That was my dream. No college, no football, no girls, none of that. Just out there, making a difference—a *real* difference."

I imagine him punching the air or slamming his hands on the table. All I can feel is the motions in the space around me that tell me he's pumped. Anyone who claims there are only five senses is shortsighted—we're sensory processing machines. Electricity charges off Chase as he shares himself with me.

"Soon as I finished high school, I signed up for basic training. Brutal for a lot of guys, but I'd been preparing. Pull-ups, push-ups, star jumps, you name it, I'd done it, every morning for years. Spent time out on the range, shooting with my brothers. Run five miles? No problem. I'd spent my life getting ready for this."

I believe him. Wasn't that always my father's mantra? Be prepared. That meant first aid kits, bleeding kits, physical fitness, and contact numbers punched into the phone. Not his wife, though. She was never prepared. Still isn't.

"The first time I wore that uniform, 'scuse me for saying, but I think I may have cried a little."

I smile at the pride in his delivery. This time I take his hand and cover it with mine.

"Ended up in the infantry, best in my division. But that wasn't what I'd had my heart set on."

"Special ops?"

"You better believe it. To be a Green Beret? No greater honor, not that I can think of. But you need to have the language, the cultural skills. I'm a dumb hick, so maybe not. If someone's relying on my linguistic ability to save the village, that village might end up going down in flames, just saying. But I want more. I do the training, make selection, end up in the Ranger regiment."

I shuffle in my seat at his words.

His voice chokes up. "That's when I found my place, my purpose in life. You know, my mama always used to talk about finding my own path in life, and I didn't always believe her. But, first day with that badge, and I knew it."

Angie dumps down my check. "Can I get you anything?"

It's as if I've vaporized. I dig in my pocket for my wallet for my card. "Thanks, Ang, we're all good." I slide the rest of my milkshake over to him. "Finish for me?"

He leans close, strokes my cheek. "If you'll finish for me later?"

My body pulses toward him. All I want is him.

"I never thought I'd find someone special. I'd always hoped, but—" He breaks away from me.

I'm still hanging onto his words which turn over in my mind. "What makes you think you've found someone special? I'm just your regular girl. I'm just like all the other girls. Nothing special about me."

"That's where you're wrong."

His hand covers mine again and I batten down against the flood of warm feelings rising up to drown me.

"You're like a book, written for me." Something wavers in those words. Dumb hick—is that how he sees himself?

"I miss reading."

He drawls. "You don't read anymore?"

I shake my head. "Haven't learned how to. And I still battle with audio. Not the same as the pages, the words on the pages…"

"All Greek to me." He whispers close in my ear. "Come home with me."

This time there's no hesitation. "Yes."

Chapter Seven

We're in his apartment, the door closed, the world shut out. I've left my mother, my future, my disability, to move with ease in this world beyond the door. It will attach itself to me the second I leave here. But for right now, I want to shut it all behind me. Allow myself these moments where I can be the Skye that I was. Someone bold, independent, laughing. Someone who took chances. Someone who was loved.

Not the Skye, who is also me, who slips and slides down that spiral.

Not the Skye who is blind, who chopped off her access to the world by trying to exit it entirely.

We're both naked.

He's turned me onto my stomach and his strong hands knead the doughiness of my ass. I sigh in voluptuous pleasure. His fingers roll up over my spine and back down again, easing away the tension I store there. Every thumb push releases, releases, releases. I am not so much clay as jelly, my solid state succumbing to liquid under his firm hands.

"I'm not hurting you, am I?"

I stretch out. "Hardly. I may never get up again."

He reaches to the bedside table for more oil. And once again, his hands grip my waist and run upward, the oil warming as he slides over its slickness.

I am in heaven. Endless, delicious heaven.

He's in no hurry. He means to know every inch of me.

I believe him.

He turns his attention to the tops of my thighs, the same rhythmic push-pull motion that triggers off an endless stream of calm.

I am borne on voluminous clouds of light, carried from drifting wakefulness to erotic lushness. His fingers brush against my wetness—and I am wet—but pass by, an incidental movement rather than the end game.

He traces a path down the centerline of my leg, over the back of my knee with its tender flesh, and up over the tough no-nonsense of my calf, tapering through to my foot.

My wrapped ankle hums in jealousy. It will not be as generously loved. No, it will have to wait for another time, another space, maybe.

The more Chase works his magician's unweaving spell on my body, the more aware I am of the frightened woman who shares my body. My muscles hold me tight, rigid, ready for fight, for I can no longer flee. Even the relative unimportance of my big toe is caught up tight with the pressure of pushing forward, keeping upright, carrying the weight of my existence in its marvel of bone, sinew, and blood. In his hands, it has momentarily dropped the fight, given in to the unlikeliness of its acknowledgement. Who of us ever really drop into the cells, the nerves, the sheer mechanics of our bodies? And thanks them for every grateful moment it offers us.

Each motion over my toes elicits a strange tingling, tickling, that is both laugh-out-loud and arousing. My response is as uncertain as a toddler's first steps.

Again he asks, "Am I hurting you?"

Somehow I cannot imagine him ever hurting me. And yet, this man who holds my body so reverently, who is making love so surely and so sweetly to all of my flesh, has ripped holes in others that can never be filled. He has taken life, of that I am sure. Yet, he is taking nothing for granted, acknowledging the full beauty of heart-beating vividness with his hands, his fingers, his intention.

He flips me over.

I am spread wide, ready, willing, open.

He resumes his exploration, back over my toes, my ankle, my shin, my knee, my thigh.

My skin buzzes, it is singing, it is a full symphony of sound waves rippling through me.

He kisses me gently on my bellybutton as he works his way over my waist, my breasts, my shoulders.

The pictured calm that the survivors' leader talks of is no longer a wistful panacea to all of my stress. For this moment, it is a reality. Who knew that the massaging of the space where the joints meet in my shoulder could be so satisfying? As if there were a pocketful of pleasure waiting to unleash itself. Almost as delicious as the feel of his thumb in the base of my palm as he rolls my wrist around.

When he finally reaches my nipples, the pleasure is almost painful. Soft brushes, no hard pinches or slight squeezes, are enough to propel me into the stratosphere. No longer am I above the clouds, I am above the earth entirely, transported into the nothingness of the universe's vast stretch.

He doesn't dwell too long on those swollen peaks.

This is not their show, merely their part. For the

first time, I am aware of my body's infinite capacity for extreme pleasure. And it's not about my nipples or my clit, which is swollen hard.

For so long I have wanted to be out of my body, to exist outside of it, barely inhabiting it at all. To be in the physical realm has tethered me to my brain's tentative neurons that underreact—or is it overreact—to the transmitters that reduce our physical experience to mere chemical reactions. I have been a prisoner in this body. I am subject to its whims, a pawn to its reactions to the senses, to food, to experience. I have only known so much pain, and the darkness that it plunges me into.

Yet, as his fingers lazily work over me, I resonate with electricity that floods so much pleasure through me. I have a kind of ease in my skin that I never thought possible. My brain is awash with all of the right kind of juice. It's delicious. Addictive. I sigh, drifting into a plateau of relaxation that straddles the waking and the unconscious.

I don't want to be anywhere else but in this body. With this man.

He stops again for the innocuous bottle of coconut oil that thankfully doesn't smell of stereotypical visits to beach islands. As he warms the oil between his hands, a slick sound of oil slapping slips through.

It mimics the sound of him inside me, my wetness sucking him in. The sound of sex.

His massage continues, this time at the folds around my clit. His fingers soften over those pink folds that are frequently overlooked in the search for the hard, round clit, the pearl in the oyster.

Even in my own explorations in the v between my thighs, I've failed to appreciate their sensitivity.

Perhaps it stands to reason, that a body that can bring forth so much pain, could have and does have the capacity for as much, if not more, pleasure. I groan, a deep guttural growl low in my throat. He has me hovering at the edge of release. But I don't want it be to be over yet. I want to get lost in this feeling forever, for as long as it takes to truly forget, to imprint a new memory.

A slippery finger glides inside me, swiftly joined by another until I ache pleasantly with fullness. He opens me wide and my muscles slacken against him. In my past, limited experience, there has been nothing pleasant about finger fucking. Crude, elementary, and without finesse, hard fingers have jabbed and jerked, searching for something they will never find with harsh and heavy. Rigid digits are not cocks with their more subtle helmetry. Somehow—and I don't care how—Chase's fingers are stroking inside me, coaxing me along, working inside me. Every few moments, a knuckle brushes my clit. I open my legs wider. The tops of his knees rest against my thighs. I arch my hips toward him as he continues with his hands.

Yet again he asks, "Am I hurting you?"

My God, no. An orgasm is building deep inside me, rippling out from where his fingers stroke me, and branching out through every nerve fiber in my body. I hang in suspended motion as those ripples push upward further higher, nudging at release then falling back again, a little more each time, a little fuller, a little riper. A noise I don't even recognize roars from me. I am animal. I am woman. I am goddess. I am life itself.

His fingers move faster, but not harsher.

My body pulls taut, an arrow poised, the target

set...I raise up, up, up. And then, it snaps. I shake. I pant. The tremors rush through me, tearing down everything in its path, levelling it to the ground, reducing it to ashes. I grab his arm and squeeze down hard, holding on, gripping tight to something, anything, to steady myself. My vagina spasms around his hand, contracting, pulsing, sucking him into me. I never used to believe in miracles, in life. I do now. I am at the universe's feet, basking in the marvel of the glory of the communion of man and woman. This. This is what love is. Love made physical. The capacity for joy.

Suddenly, the sensitivity bites back at me. I push away his hand as my throbs subside. No more. My body can handle no more. Not now. And yet, how much it can handle. That much capacity for fuckyeah. A fleeting thought—had I succeeded, I would never have known this. I tuck that away. Now is not the time.

He still kneels between my open thighs, his fingers lovingly brushing over my pubic hair, my stomach, my thighs. He stops and kisses my knee before taking my hand and kissing it, holding it, resting it still against his cheek.

My breathing resumes. I am spent. I'd heard that word before but never appreciated it. Spent. I have nothing more to give here, to offer. Nothing left—spent. For all that I have opened up here, he has gifted back to me a thousandfold.

I pull him down toward me, my stickiness still on his hand. We kiss; the heat of his body closes the space between us. My legs remain open to him, my body open to him. And yet, he asks for nothing in return. No hints for blowjobs, or hands pushed down into groins, or crass body humping.

He just kisses me over and over. "Skye, you are so beautiful to me."

I believe him. My hands tighten on his shoulders.

"You have no idea how beautiful you are to me."

The words are spoken with such reverence, I am humbled in their presence. That they are about me caresses my burned-out spirit.

"Thank you for sharing with me."

I stroke his face, feel his stubble. "I have done nothing but lie here."

He pauses. "No. You have given yourself to me, and it is beautiful."

Certainly, I have given my body. Do I even have anything else to give? Immediately, my thoughts turn to the mess of my life that resides six floors up.

I can't stay with my mother.

He tucks his body alongside mine, our hands interlinked, a leg casually thrown over mine. It's warmth and togetherness.

I remind myself it's temporary. I have to ask. "Don't you want me to do something to you?"

"No pressure." He curls in closer. "Are you happy?"

"I'm certainly satisfied."

"Then I'm happy. All I want is for you to be happy."

His words weigh heavily.

"My love." I stroke his arm that's wrapped around me. "I can't even make me happy, I would never ask for you to take on that burden. It's not for you to make me happy."

There's no response to that, only the silent lifting of his chest as he breathes in.

I venture the question. "Are you happy?"

He shifts. "I am grateful. Grateful to be here, in bed, with a beautiful woman who calms my soul."

If he's lying or riffing off sweet nothings, it's hard to tell. Is it because I want to believe what he says? Or is it because I can detect no sugary syrup in his tone?

He continues, "I see couples every day. Most of them are not talking to each other. Not even noticing that the other is there. Kind of existing together. I don't know whether they fuck or not, but I'd guess not. There's no sweetness between them."

"That's probably because once the honeymoon period's worn off, the magic's gone. I wouldn't know."

"Yeah, could be. But I get the feeling the magic was never there. Like they missed something somewhere." He stops then.

Maybe he's said too much. A military man with a romantic streak that burns hot and heavy. Not too far a stretch, I guess. Both loving and fighting give the false impression that there's something worth hoping for, a better future, a brighter future, a warmer, fuzzier something that you can maybe, just about reach. But that something keeps on moving, and you keep on chasing. I keep on chasing. Chase. "Tell me about your tattoos."

"My ink? I got a mean-assed skull, right here, on my right arm. Got that one after my first tour. Workmanship's pretty good on that one. Yeah, says *death before dishonor*." He pauses.

A shutter slides down between us. It's as if I can hear his mind working, as he gets lost inside his head. I press. "My dad had one of those memorial tattoos. It was a gun in a pair of boots, the helmet resting on the end of the gun. Never said a word about it."

He takes my hand and runs my finger against the inside of his biceps. "Names of two of my best friends. Finest men you'd ever meet. Never forget." Another pause. "You see guys walking around with some ink they have no business wearing. Gotta earn it. Can't just get wasted and take things you didn't earn. See young guys, teens, with a Navy SEAL frog. Ain't right."

He rolls over onto his back. "If there's one day I replay over and over, it's my last day in the field. Maybe if I'd taken a little more time? Been a little more certain? What if I'd just followed procedure as I'd done hundreds, thousands of times before? I knew the drill. Knew my role. Knew the risks. But, shit, something said, wait, hang on, cause for deviation. The whole setup looked standard. Hostages in the building, hostiles here, here, and here. Guys get in, neutralize, get out. You know, I go over and over and over that setup. What the hell made my gut twitch? The only answer I come up with was this kid crying. Shit, sounded like a kid crying. Guess what? Wasn't a fucking kid crying."

My hand rests on his chest. His heart thumps and bumps under my palm.

He's half-talking to me, half to himself, marking out the same territory over and over, looking for the angle that's been overlooked, that will click his world back into place. There is no angle.

"Who the fuck follows their intuition? You follow your orders, you rely on your training. You're prepared, you're tactically engaged, you follow through on the procedure you've executed a thousand times before. It ain't fucking rocket science. In an unpredictable environment, you rely on your own and your team's predictability."

The heat from him crackles and fizzes with frustration. Anger. Recrimination. His body tenses, his heart thumping faster.

How awful and how wonderful is the human mind? A master and commander of our emotions, our bodies, always tripping us up with visual and audio replays, distorted over time, of our greatest failures. What we didn't do, what we did wrong, what we should have done, what we could have done. A marvel of never-ending torture, all self-inflicted.

Chase can never be back outside that house, making a different decision, no matter how much his brain wills him to do so. It's over.

"They let me go with an honorable discharge. That's it. Everything I worked for, dreamed of, gone. Because I followed a hunch. Not my team, not my training, not my own orders. All fucking gone. I won't ever be out there with my guys again. Never. I'm a thirty-eight-year-old civilian. Who fixes faucets and calls out for repairmen. And even that's because my uncle's about to bite the big one." His hand covers mine. "And then I meet you. And you gave me something to believe in again. When I'm with you, I feel...calm. Like my demons can't find a space to start ripping and clawing."

It's my turn to tense. "You don't even know me."

"I know you're kind, you're gentle, you're soft." His voice is steady.

Isn't this everything I wanted, once upon a time, for a man to tell me? Or was it everything I wanted to be able to tell a man? For him to rescue me?

"I know I don't want to let you go."

"But one day, you might have to."

"I don't want to lose you."

Part of me has already fled through the front door. *Let you go. Lose you.* Fighting talk. The other? "Do you want to stay here? Fixing things?"

"No. There's this gym, a boxing gym, up for sale. Figured I could put in an offer, fix it up a little, offer something solid to guys who're serious about their training. I've got the experience, that's for sure."

"Sounds like a great idea."

He draws a breath. "It's back home."

My stomach twists. I swallow. "That sounds really great. You should put in that offer. I bet they'd be really glad to have someone like you down there."

"Plenty of us everywhere. No one really looking." His tone shoots down anything that might look like hope.

I pack up my heart, piece by piece from where it's shattered. Him gone? Far south, like a bird that flees from the winter.

"You can always come with me, you know."

"I did just come with you." He pokes me in my ribs, hitting that sweet spot that makes me jump sky-high.

"Real cute."

"You better believe it." The tension breaks. I can't stay with my mother. But I can't stay with Chase either. Would it be so bad to take a chance and climb in alongside him and journey? Would it?

Chase doesn't need to take on my need.

"It's only been days, but I love you, my girl."

His words gut punch me. I mumble, slide away from him. "I've got to get back. I should have been back hours ago." I'm on the wrong side of the bed, my clothes somewhere here in the dark. I scrabble about over the bedclothes.

"Wait, I'll get it for you." The bedsprings squeak as he moves. "Here."

When he undressed me, he didn't rip or tear, but he slowly disrobed me. What he's handed me now is a pile of perfectly folded clothes. A lump lodges in my throat. *Love you, my girl.*

I dress, acutely aware of his eyes on me. Of all the words to choose. They're just words. But, they're *those* words. The words that have me as a dartboard to my mother's need. Couldn't he have said nothing? Idle chats about futures and dreams had no place with words like love. Love didn't cure all.

"My most beautiful."

Could he stop already?

He brings my crutches to me.

I want to scream. I cannot get out of there fast enough and yet I move as though I've been accosted by wet cement. I trip over my own feet. I stumble over non-existent levels in the floor. Tension pushes behind my skin, urging me forward faster. But I'm wading.

He kisses me at the door.

When I'm standing in his arms, like this, I can't find the need for distance, but rather, its opposite.

"Think about what I said." He strokes my hair. "I can't stay in someone else's home, someone else's job, forever. This here is temporary. And since I met you, I feel my future clicking into place."

"I don't think it's with me, Chase."

"You're beautiful, intelligent, kind, gentle, did I mention beautiful?" Each superlative is punctuated with a kiss.

He smells so good I want to dissolve in him. But it's still too much. Words are words are words. They have no value in of themselves. Anyone can say anything and mean nothing at all. *Love you, my girl.* Why those words?

"When I'm with you, I feel like I have purpose again," he says. "Let me walk you back."

I unravel from him. Alone, I head back along the block's spine to the broken elevator.

I can't stay with my mother. *Love you, my girl.*

But I can't go with him either.

Chapter Eight

The trek up the stairs breaks me. Halfway up, I sit down, right where I am. Neither up, nor down, haven't there been any number of songs about sitting here? My ankle stings. I visualize kicking that cast against the stair's edge, causing it to shatter into a billion pieces, freeing me to move again.

Somehow, I get back to the apartment.

I let myself in and am overwhelmed at the smell of lamb roasting. It spits and crackles as my mother takes it out of the oven.

"Did I miss your birthday?"

My mother clucks back at me. "Can't I make myself roast lamb if I feel like it?"

"You can do whatever you want."

"I fancied it." She huffs and puffs as she lifts the tray back into the oven.

It really does smell good. She's added rosemary and wine. Lots of wine.

"I thought I'd make some potatoes too. They'll be done in another half hour or so."

I can't stay with my mother. But maybe it wouldn't be so bad if I did. She's made dinner. She means well. I don't have a cookie-cutter mother; who does?

"Sounds great, Ma."

My mother moves around the kitchen, a hive of activity. "I also stopped by the bakery and picked up something for dessert. Apple pie, your favorite."

I refrain from saying that pecan is my favorite. Apple is hers.

"There's some white in the fridge if you want a glass."

Wrong-footed, I slide back into her trap. "Sure."

"Let me get it for you."

"Thank you."

She hurries past me, trailing the scents of smoke, ashes, and rosemary. The fridge opens and a bottle clunks down on the counter. She scrabbles about for a corkscrew. "It's in here somewhere, where are you?"

Not for the first time, I'm grateful that I can never be called upon to look for things that are right in front of her. The scrabbling picks up, then the drawer slams and another whooshes open.

"Can't find it. It must be in here somewhere."

On the stove, a pot boils over, the hot water rushing over the edge and hissing as it hits the plate.

My mother mutters. "Corkscrew, corkscrew."

I move toward the stove only to collide into her. "Sorry."

She snaps back. "I'm only going to take a second. You have no patience."

"The pot."

A beat. "Shit, shit, shit." A clang and a clank as she moves and shifts. More hissing, then the bubble boil of water. "Broccoli's a little overdone."

The wine sits forgotten.

"I'm going to move out."

I don't know which of us is more stunned at my proclamation.

"What?"

"I think I should move out." My second iteration holds more doubt than my first. Why do I fold so easily to her? I straighten my shoulders, ready to catch my future with both hands this time. "I am going to move out. It's time."

"Did something happen at your group this morning? Did you talk about me?"

The clanging and clinking of the work of cooking carries on. Slower this time, as though she's processing what I'm saying.

"No, Ma, we didn't talk about you." I steady my voice so as not to show the irritation. Why does she think it's about her? Always about her. "I've been here long enough, under your feet—"

"It's no problem. Don't you think you better get yourself sorted first? Financially, are you even in a position to find your own place?"

I grit my teeth. "No, probably not. But I've got work coming in, it's steady, reliable. And I can always find something smaller, or maybe a room to rent."

"A room?"

"You know what I mean."

The oven door cranks open and a tray bangs down on the counter, the fat sizzling and spitting in the pan. She slams the door shut. "Is this anything to do with him?"

"There's no him, I keep telling you that."

"If your father knew that—"

"Dad's dead, remember?"

The drawer opens. A second later, the crisscrossing of blade against sharpener as she readies the knife for the lamb that's long since been slaughtered. "I hate carving the fucking meat. Your father used to do this.

110

When he was here. Now it's up to me to change the light bulbs, make the money, carve the meat. Fuck."

Any joy has sapped out of her.

Guilt twitches up my spine as I breathe in the aroma of the dinner that she claims is for me. That I can't help carve the meat or change the light bulbs settles between her words. It's always there. How I can't help her look for things or comment on how cute some TV star is. And I never will be able to. Not anymore. Not like I used to. "I'm sorry, Ma."

"Where are you going to go? Have you given it any thought?"

"Not yet." The thought swims about uneasily in my stomach. "But it will be good for me to stand on my own feet."

"Don't you think you should make a few plans first and then head out there? You're going to have to do things differently now."

"I know."

"Maybe give it a few months, get yourself sorted."

Her words make sense. What was I thinking? I can't leave. She knows what's best for me. And she's right. Ducks have to be lined up in ponds and all of that. Or squirrels on dance floors. I'm high on Chase's lust, that's all. And his words, his words that run a loop in my mind. The unease in my gut abates.

The plates chime as they're taken down from their cupboard.

"How much meat do you want?"

None is my automatic answer. "Two, please."

There's a scratch of metal on ceramic as she does the dishing up.

There's no suggestion that we sit at the dining

room table. That space is reserved for my mother's sewing machine that's all threaded and ready with no foot ever going to push on that pedal. Laundry takes up the rest of the space.

Instead, I follow my mother into the lounge.

The TV is already on. It's a makeover show. One of those ones where they rip apart some volunteers' wardrobe, then make them over into something more acceptable, more uniform. This afternoon's unlucky candidate is from Ohio and likes to wear studded dog collars, leather skirts, and deep lipstick.

"Can you believe what some people look like?" My mother tut-tuts at the screen. "Visions of loveliness." Her knife and fork scrape over her plate with each mouthful. Her own wine tumbler makes a regular journey from coffee table to mouth and back again.

"Maybe she's happy with the way she looks? Maybe it says something about her?"

A grunt. "Yeah. That she's a slob. And that skirt? It's maybe two inches from her business. In my day, we didn't wear skirts like that unless we were looking for trouble." She takes a bite. "You used to wear your skirts too short."

I protest. "They always came to my knee."

"Yeah, too short. You don't have the right kind of knees for skirts. Stick to pants rather."

I finish the dry meat, the oily potatoes, and the waterlogged broccoli. "Thanks, Ma, that was great."

"Maybe you can do a lasagna for tomorrow's dinner?"

"Sure."

I hop back into the kitchen, my empty plate in my

hand. Everything's back to normal. I'll cook tomorrow, we'll watch TV, and I'll do my work during the week and head to my meetings on Saturdays.

I find that white wine resting on the counter where she's abandoned it. I feel two drawers down, open one, and dip my hand in. A corkscrew shape is easy to find. Two seconds later, the corkscrew in hand, I wrestle with the bottle.

Her voice calls from the lounge. "Skye? Bring me some more red, please. And can you start loading the dishwasher? I want to let it run tonight."

Shit.

By the time I return to the lounge, my hands, despite the rubber gloves, slip and slide with lamb grease. The dishwasher hums and whirs, the bigger pans stacked up in the rack.

"You forgot my wine."

Shit.

I turn back into the kitchen. A thought nags, pulls and drags at me. *This is what it's like, remember?* I discard the thought. Her red wine stash waits near the fridge. I pull out a bottle from the three that remain.

"Skye, you're missing the big reveal."

My standing leg protests—too much time on my feet. I sink to my knees, bottle in hand, and crawl back into the lounge.

"Look what they've done to her. I wouldn't go for that screaming-red color but it's so much better than what it was. You think?"

I dump her bottle down, then shimmy climb up to where my glass of wine waits.

"And I'm not sure that blue is the best on her. Not that shade at least, that petrol blue. Pretty sure I've got a dress that color. Do you remember that one?"

The metal stays crick-click open as she unscrews her second bottle of the evening. "The blue looks nice with that white jacket of mine."

This is what it will be like. Her and me. We'll watch what she wants to on TV. She'll talk to me as if I can see the backdrops, marvel at the costumes, gasp in wonder at the special effects or the car chases. She'll drink her wine and I'll drink mine. She'll talk about her day. I'll cook the dinner. And she'll sit on her butt while I clean it all up again.

Is that enough of a life?

It has been for two years now.

It has been enough.

Is it still enough?

Is it even enough if I can sneak out downstairs and wrap up in him for a few hours? A few moments in which I feel alive again?

The show finishes and the next starts up. Something about how to improve your cooking. All of these shows are about how to be better; how to look better, how to make your home better, how to cook, eat, speak, anything and everything better. It squats like a toad on everything I have pieced together to be functional, forget good.

My mother pulls her finger on the pin and tosses her grenade. "You can't leave. I lost my job, remember?"

Chapter Nine

Sunday afternoon, I head downstairs. We've run out of milk. Ma's already a few glasses of wine down, so guess who's the lucky person to hit the store? The elevator works again, who knows for how long. I've travelled down two flights when he gets in.

I can't miss that intoxicating scent of him, it fills me up, has me wanting more. I brush aside our last meeting—it can wait. Instead, I smile. "Going down?"

The elevator door closes.

He stands close to me as we wait for the initial dip as the elevator heads south. His hand slides up the back of my thigh and cups my ass, squeezing and kneading.

I turn toward him, my hand firm over the front of his jeans.

He groans.

I smile again. "Because I'd like to go down on you."

He makes an appreciative sound. "Right here? Right now?"

"Can you think of a better place?"

We reach the ground floor. The elevator bounces before the door opens. There's no sound of footsteps, of rushing, of people sucking up the air.

He leans forward and sends the elevator back upward. Then he hits the stop.

I'm not as agile as I'd like to be, but I can do this,

here, in a stopped elevator with him. I push him back against the wall. No time for preamble. I unbuckle his belt, undo his jean's button and unzip his fly, releasing the hardness that's curled up in his jockeys. I slide downward until I can easily take him in my mouth.

He steadies himself against the elevator's wall, his hands lightly resting on my head.

He tastes like soap and salt, and his balls rest comfortably in my hand. I suck him ruthlessly, leaving no spare moment for teasing or taunting—that can happen later when we have the luxury of time. I work my tongue against his penis, against the underside of his head where the skin bunches together, his sweet spot that lifts him off. The faster I lap my tongue, my lips sliding up and down, the more his abdomen contracts, his balls lift, and his panting increases. What I wouldn't give to make a little eye contact with him. To let him know, eye-to-eye that I love the power I have over him at this moment to bring him pleasure, to take his vulnerability in my mouth and take care of it. To let him know that I love it, love him. Love him?

I lick and suck, my hand working his shaft.

He grips me tightly.

Then he comes in thick, salty spurts that I lap up, my hand catching the excess. His groans are music to my ears. I bring him back down again, softer, slower, briefer kisses on his cock that's still hard. I lick up the cum, removing the evidence.

He regains his breath and pulls me upward, his mouth crushing down on mine. He kisses me as if he were a thirsty man.

His cum is in my mouth, in my hands.

His words lift me up. "You are amazing, Skye."

No, you are. He has flipped my world on its axis, shown me a door that I couldn't see for looking. I kiss him back, my tongue speaking the language my voice can't.

He comes back up for air. "Wait until I get you in my bed. I want to repay the favor."

"No favor."

He holds up my hand. "I don't have a tissue for you."

"I'll make a plan."

"You are so special to me, Skye." He holds me close.

The heat from his body never ceases to entice me. How can he burn so hot and not be in perpetual flames? Or maybe it's the heat I feel when I'm around him. I'm on fire.

All of me is awake. Alive. Burning through the layers of self that are no longer me. He did that for me.

"Wouldn't it be great if we could stay here forever, the two of us, suspended in mid-air?"

I laugh. It would be great. "We might get hungry."

"I know what I'd like to eat."

The rush of blood to my groin is immediate. I know what I'd like him to eat, too.

He kisses me again, gentler this time. He cups my head in his hands and drenches me in tenderness. It's almost too much.

"What do you want from me, Chase?"

"Nothing. Everything. You. Whatever you can give."

I wait for a tentacle of need to unleash and wrap itself around me, but nothing happens.

He restarts the elevator and we sink back down to

the ground floor.

****

I don't go to him that night.

Love you, my girl. His words still ring in my ears. Give me blow jobs in elevators any day—far less messy, far less complicated. Sex, pure sex. How long can I trot that line out and still believe it?

"Package here for you," yells my mother. Her first day at home. No job. No work. She hunkers down in the kitchen, fluffing out the papers, tinkering with her laptop. Applying for jobs or your regular surfing? Smoke fugs the apartment.

I reek of it. It's in my hair, my clothes, my pores.

The cardboard-wrapped package elicits a childish delight. Is it really for me? It's heavy, compact.

"You order something?" My mother's voice is bored.

"Not that I can remember."

I peel off the packing tape, open up the dusty-feeling card, and pick up something that's plastic—a DVD? And, a book. I flip open the book. Instead of smooth and slick, there are raised bumps. My heart quickens. Braille. There're not one, but two DVDs.

My mother comes and stands beside me. "Took you enough time."

I gather up the box and its contents and flee to my room's privacy. Chase. Must be. Has to be. Didn't I mention reading? He was listening. He heard me. I find my phone by my bed. It strikes me—I've never asked for his number nor has he asked for mine. Unlike previous anythings, there's been no texting. No late night messaging. No notes.

Old school style courting. Courting? *Love you, my*

girl.

I tear off the plastic packaging of one of the DVD cases and pull it open. I slide the CD into my laptop. A second's wait before a woman's voice floods the room. I open the book and begin with the introductory chapter.

My mother's voice intrudes. "Have you finished your work, yet?"

I don't pause the CD. "All done."

"Don't you want to help me with this?"

"What?"

"This?"

I shut off the CD. "*What*?"

Her tone slaps me about the face. "Sorry, are you busy?"

"Not at all," I snap back.

My mother walks toward me, her feet slipping over the wood floor, her perfume cloud invading the room. "It's all tangled in on itself."

She dumps a mass of neck chains into my hand.

"I wanted to wear my cross. I have an interview this afternoon. But it's got all caught up with the other. I really should hang up a nail or something."

The chains clump together in a ball—only a few stubborn loops have escaped. "How many are in here?"

"Three." Then she adds, "Two gold, and then the one silver."

"Makes no difference to me."

She huffs, sitting next to me, causing the mattress to dip and my new CD case to tumble to the ground.

I reach down and fumble for the case that fell, retrieve it. I'm sitting with my package and its contents all strewn around me. How does she not see me? How does she not hear me?

"Estelle's friend, Mike—"

Her voice thickens and I can guess who she met up with on Friday.

"—he has this little place out by the lake. Says we can go visit it some time."

I don't need to know braille to read between those lines.

"I was thinking this weekend, but I can't leave you by yourself. You don't want to come with me, do you?"

You don't want to come with me. Interesting collection of words. I don't. "I've got another set of interviews coming through from the embassy. They're looking for a new diplomat—"

"That's what I explained to Mike—he called me this morning—I said that you'd probably be busy so you probably wouldn't be able to make it. He understands that I can't leave you alone."

"Yes, you can. I'll be fine."

"What if there's a fire?"

"I'll smell it." If I can smell when Cherry Jubilee's let one rip in the foyer, I'm pretty sure I could smell something in flames. "Go, enjoy yourself."

"It's about time I had some enjoyment in my life."

I run my fingers over the tangle, searching out loose threads. "Isn't there an easy way to do this? Can't we search online or something?"

"But you're so good at this." A beat. "I'll tell him yes, then?"

"Who?"

"You're not even listening. Why do I bother—"

"The friend, Mike, the lake, this weekend, go." I know she's already said yes. There's silence as I attempt the impossible task in front of me. A whole weekend without her. *With him.* The things we could do with a whole weekend. A voluptuous me unfolds inside, replete with the pleasure that could come my way.

She fidgets away beside me, fumbling about with stripped-off masking tape. "Aren't you going to ask me about it then?"

"About what?"

"The interview!" She tosses the tape, and the bed bounces, causing my grip to slip.

I grit my teeth. "Tell me about the interview, then."

"It's at an animal shelter. I'd be perfect for it. They're looking for loving, caring people who love animals. Can you think of a better job for me?"

"What about another paralegal job?"

"I've always wanted to work with animals. So much nicer than humans." A pause. "Is it coming along?"

This is how it's going to be. Every day, for the rest of my life.

"I'm going to move out." I say it again. "As soon as I can find something, I'm moving out."

"We already talked about this—you're not ready to move out. And, I can't afford to be without income at the moment."

"Ma, you have an interview later today. Maybe you'll get the job?"

"It doesn't pay as well as my last job."

I point out the obvious. "You're not going to be here this weekend."

"That's different. It's for two days. You need someone with you most of the time. You're not very independent, you know."

The conversation stirs up any doubts and fears I have, whips them up into a sundae of panic and hands it over to me, complete with frosting. I refuse to eat it, though. I can't. How much longer can I live on pause? Flying in a holding pattern above my own life, waiting to either come in to land or fly off in another direction? But circling, circling, circling, waiting. Enough. It's enough.

"I'll get a seeing eye dog. Lots of people do that."

"And what happens when you have one of your…episodes? What if you forget your medication?"

I stop with the pretense that I'm unwinding her chains. "I have Razia and the group. I haven't come off my meds and I probably never will. And most days I walk a bit, too. Maybe I'll join a gym as well." Chase will have a gym one day. Oh, yeah.

She yanks the chains from me. "You're useless at this. I'll go see if there are any ideas online."

The room sighs as she leaves. It's the same relief as stepping off a rollercoaster. No more of the up-down, up-up, down-up unpredictability.

I want to choose calm. Something steady, predictable, something like that feeling I get when I'm with him. Of shelter, of a home that's unlike anything I've experienced before. She's always been like this. It used to be bad when Dad was away from home—she'd disappear for hours on 'weekends away', leaving a perfume trail of broken hearts behind her.

I pick up the how-to book Chase sent me. My mother would balk at such a gift. Where was the romance? The luxuriousness? The expense? I want to, need to, thank him.

But it's Monday morning. He'll be busy with the

administration of his super-ing.

I pull a sheet of paper from my printer and find a pen. Anytime I write, I'm reminded of high school art classes where the teacher asked us to keep our pencils on the paper, and our gaze on the subject. We'd draw without looking down. Now it doesn't matter where I look. I scribble out a few lines.

I resist the urge to apply lipstick and kiss the paper. What use is a lipstick smudge? What I want is to slide back into his arms, to cuddle up into him, and feel the world recede. Maybe that's what my mother wanted all those times? To be held and never let go of. To have her man with her, not fighting for causes.

Love you, my girl.

Chase is leaving. And what of my own future…without him?

I open up the appropriate function on my laptop. My voice is clear as I request the guide dogs association.

Chapter Ten

Three more sleeps, two more sleeps, one more sleep. I count down the nights until I have him all to me. A whole weekend, all to me.

He's been snowed under with burst geysers and flooded basements.

I can wait. I've waited two years. We've stolen kisses in the gaps under the stairs, screwed like teenagers up against his bedroom wall and brushed past each other in corridors. He's addictive.

Friday arrives and I'm bubbling over with excitement. I can't keep it contained no matter how hard I try. It unstoppers and fizzes out everywhere.

The more he touches me, the more I want to be touched. It's like a switch has turned on that has no 'off' switch, that's been dimmed for too long.

"Where's the suitcase?"

My mother's voice intrudes on my reverie. "I have no idea. Top of your cupboard?"

She's a whirlwind of nervousness. "Mike called."

I gear up for the he's-not-coming, the we-have-to-postpone.

"He's coming by early to fetch me."

There was an option I didn't consider. Razia's suggestion that I tend to see the negative in everything comes to mind. "It's probably in the hallway cupboard."

She stomps back and forth down the passageway, preparing and re-preparing what she's taking.

I put my earphones in and switch my brain to think in French. It's not the same as thinking in English or Italian or Spanish. The way words take shape in conversations are different. The sentence's structure shifts meaning. I consider how they say they're missing something. I don't miss Chase, but rather he misses me. *Il me manques.* No longer do I sound mournful or needy, but adored, loved, sore from absence.

I wrap myself up in my work, secure that this evening I will head downstairs for the entire night and wake up in his arms tomorrow. He's said as much. *Il me manques.* I turn the words over in my mind, letting them wash over me as the French ambassador talks of climate control.

She's back in my room, that pacing upsetting my flow.

"Skye, you will remember to take the trash out, right? And to latch the door behind you? I don't want anything to happen here."

"Unlikely. Six floors with an intermittent elevator?"

"If someone's determined to get in, they will."

"We have nothing of any value."

"There's the TV."

Heaven forbid someone takes off with that. "It'll be fine. Go and enjoy yourself."

Her voice settles. "I can't tell you how much I'm looking forward to this weekend. It's been a long time since I had some time to myself, you know? Not having to worry about anything."

I've long since switched off my recording. "Relax,

Ma, it will be fine."

"After your father—Mike's nice."

"Glad to hear it."

She loiters half-in, half-out of my bedroom, but doesn't say whatever is clearly on her mind. "I'll leave you his number in case you need to call."

"You're not taking your phone?"

"I am, but just in case."

"Right."

I have no doubt she'll write the numbers by the main phone in the kitchen, so I can access it easily with my nonexistent sight. Now's not the time to remind her.

She flibberty-gibbets back out to her own room. Somewhere a radio's playing a crooner who's singing of lost love.

There's a knock at our door.

My mother remains ensconced in her packing. There's another knock.

"Who is that, I wonder?" My mother says but she still makes no move toward the door.

I undo my earphones and clamber off the bed.

She meets me in the hall. "I wonder who that could be?"

If you opened the fucking door, you'd find out, an alternate me yells at her. In this universe though, I undo the latch and swing open the door.

That smell—lemony, tart, and crisp, like a dip in a fjord. I freeze.

"Hey, Skye." His voice is treacle and smolder.

How much did I love that smolder? My words falter as my brain hurries to catch up to my body's immediate recognition. Funny that—how quickly the body responds, how slowly the brain, like lightning that waits for its accompanying thunder. "Brock, that's not you?"

"In the flesh, honey."

There's a sharp intake of breath behind me.

"What the hell are you doing here? You head back out, you hear me?"

I am still processing. Brock. Here. In front of me. Far from where I'd left him. Only that wasn't right—far from where he'd left me. "What are you doing here, Brock?" I repeat my mother's words. "There's nothing more to say to you." I close the door but he's done that foot-in-the-jamb trick.

"I know you must hate me. I heard about what happened and I couldn't let you—"

My mother's voice is shrill behind me. "You were clear about where you stood, you bastard. Get out of here before I call 911. Actually, I'm going to do that now." She disappears into the kitchen.

He's scrabbling now, I can hear his pace step up.

"Please, Skye. You know I didn't have a choice. And, oh, shit, I heard about you and the blind thing, I didn't believe it. But it's true. This wasn't because of what—"

My mother's voice squeaks with excitement. "I've called them and they're dispatching a vehicle. Don't think your fancy pants uniform is going to get you out of this one."

He pleads; it's almost a whine. "Please, Skye. I only want to talk."

I open my mouth.

"You've done enough."

"Ma!" I tilt my head up to where I remember Brock's eyeline is. He can look at me eyeball to eyeball. "I'll let you talk. Half an hour, no more. Wait outside."

My mother's protests start up again.

"Call the dispatchers and tell them it's been resolved."

"Are you mad? After what he did?"

To Brock, I am firm. "I'll give you half an hour."

I turn back toward my bedroom to find my purse. What had Razia said about my finding the negative? All of the effervescence that had been me that morning has drained out. I was wrong. She was wrong. Good things happen to other people. Not me. Brock is a reminder of that.

All those meetings with the survivors haven't prepared me for this. We look forward together. We don't anticipate the past showing up and asking for coffee.

I readjust my crutches and swing through as imperiously as I can muster. He cannot know that he won. "Ma, I'll be at TJ's. I'll be half an hour."

She's as bitter as a poison. "You don't owe him anything."

"No, you're right, I don't." But he owes me.

She slams the door behind us.

He walks at a clipped pace, his aftershave that temporarily blocked all of my senses weaving its spell around me.

"You look good, Skye."

Those words fuel my fire. He's surprised. Was he expecting a shallow shell of a person? Someone who'd sunk further deeper into my own brain's misfirings? Hey, I wouldn't be the first, but the way he says it rankles me. How dare he comment so casually on how I look when my stare is permanently blank, my ankle wrapped in plaster?

His shoes clop-clop-clop in syncopated rhythm. "I really was sorry to hear about what happened." A note of contrition.

I snap. "Don't think about it."

****

"Another one, Skye. How'd you do it?"

Angie's greeting grates on me. Would she like to change places? I'll gladly swap. "Two coffees." I slide into my booth that's mercifully free.

As soon as I'm settled, my crutches by my side, I shoot. "Say what you want to say, then go, got it?"

"Jeez, Skye, you don't let up an inch."

"No, I don't."

"Guess that's why you were always so good in the field. I remember that time we had that interrogation and you—"

I cut him short. "Is this a trip down memory lane? Because I don't remember climbing into that particular wagon."

He sucks in his breath. "Is it wrong to remember the good times?"

"Wrong? No. But I'm not interested."

"This is going to be more difficult than I thought." He says the words in a rush, under his breath, a mutter. Something that he can't say out loud but can't not say either.

Yes, this will be difficult for him. I refuse to give him anything more.

There's a pause as Angie brings our coffee.

"I can't remember if you take cream or not? Shall I pour?"

"I like it black."

"Right."

I refrain from adding that I could pour cream myself. It would give him the upper hand. In a power struggle, you don't give way. You keep on top. My daddy used to tell me that all the time. And believe me, you don't *not* want to be on top. Ever.

But that he wants to pour the cream for me? That he's forgotten I like it black? He's already positioning himself on this particular chessboard. Sizing me up, making his moves.

"It must be difficult for you."

His words lay there like a dead duck shot down by a poacher. What does he want me to say? No, it's a challenge. A breeze. Or yes, of course it is.

"Brock. You have a half hour that's dwindled to twenty minutes. If you want to spend it asking stupid questions, be my guest, really. But that's not the Brock I know. So cut to the chase." The second I use that expression, my cheeks redden. Shit.

He misinterprets. "Are you still sad that I ended our relationship? It was the best—"

"No. I've never regretted that."

He's searching my face for cues for lying.

I know, I used to do that, too. And he's right, I was the best at interrogation. Asking questions is one thing, it was the reading of the answers that used to intrigue me. How the lying body moves, the flicking of the eyes, the slight contraction of the muscles, the thin film of sweat. Tiny signals.

I elaborate, savoring each word. "What I regret is that I entered into a relationship with you at all."

He swallows. "I can understand why you'd say

that."

"Can you? Can you really?" I push away my coffee mug and lean closer to him. I don't want him to miss a single word. "You betrayed me. You abused my position for your own ends and threw me under a bus the second you were caught."

"That's not what happened—"

I throw my hand up between us. "Are you denying that you, a junior officer, did not deliberately and relentlessly pursue a private relationship with your commanding officer for personal gain?"

"But, that's not how—"

"Answer the question." I close the space between us. "I will never be enlisted in the military again. What exactly would I do for them? Work with the sniffer dogs? Handle their surveillance? What I deserve is a little truth, don't you agree?"

He sips his coffee, leans back from me.

I press. "What really brought you here? A guilty conscience? Or something else?"

"I didn't think this was how it would turn out."

"Enlighten me. How did you think it was going to turn out?" I wait a beat. "And be straight with me. You can turn and walk out of here and I will literally never see you again. I can't see you squirming in your seat or rolling your eyes or flipping that sugar packet over and over."

He stops with the flipping. "They used to call you The Confessor, you know that? No one got the results you did." He sounds almost wistful.

The awe in his voice disturbs the vault in my mind labelled 'before.' I dismiss his compliment that's too little, way, *way* too late. "War's not a pretty business. It needs results."

"Then you understand that for a junior officer hungry to ascend, the results justify the means?"

To hear him say it out loud is somehow cathartic. I should have recognized the signs back then. His ambition. His never-ending open mouth of ambition that devoured everything in sight. "What rank are you now?"

"Lieutenant."

"Congratulations."

He misses the sarcasm. "It means a lot to hear you say that." He picks up the sugar packet again and starts with the flip, flip, flip. "I was sorry to hear about your dad. He was one of the best."

I don't say anything, I'm clutching a raft that's being tossed over emotional rapids.

"The Green Berets are still the best. You wanted to go for that, didn't you? That was your dream?" He chucks that out so casually. "To be the first woman to pass the Q course?"

He says it knowing that as slim as my chances were then, they're totally non-existent now. Salt on vinegar on acid on an open wound.

"If anyone could have done it, it probably would have been you."

"Fuck you, Brock. Fuck you."

I don't have to ask for the time to know his is up. I dump down a few dollars and gather my crutches.

He admits. "I don't know why I came."

"I do." I stand above him. "To ease your conscience. To make sure that it wasn't really your behavior that triggered anything…unfortunate."

His fingers brush over me, cold, long and grasping.

"I loved you—you were my girl. You know that, right?"

Love you, my girl.

There may be some truth in that—isn't that why he's here? Men like him don't say sorry. His sorry changes nothing. It's dredged up memories that I'd spent so much time burying.

"I don't know anything of love, Brock. You taught me that."

I don't know if he watched me walk out or not, and quite frankly I don't care if he did or didn't. There was a time when he was all that mattered. That was a long time ago.

I ease my way back out of TJ's, onto the busy street. Usually the blaring, trumpeting noise disorients me. Today, it is calming; it is familiar. It's a marker of how far I've come. I will never be that woman again. The one who folded for a man like Brock.

By the time I reach the apartment, my mother's all set for her rendezvous with the mysterious Mike. "And?"

"And what?" I flop down on the couch. I barely paused for breath on my way back up here.

"And, what happened? What did he want? How did he even know where to find you?"

"I didn't ask him. Did you find your suitcase?"

"Why not?" She clicks her tongue. "You should've asked him that."

"I didn't."

"Do you think he's here to pick up *that guy*?" She emphasizes guy as if it were a rabid parasite or homicidal maniac. She means Chase. He's *that guy*.

"I have no idea why Brock was here, or how he got

here or where he's going from here. And I don't care."

"You shouldn't have gone with him at all. Didn't he do enough damage? When I think of your career, how it was wasted, and for what? *Him*? He wasn't fit to lick your father's boots. Or yours, for that matter."

"It's past now. Let it go."

"Did you tell him that he was responsible?"

My voice is peppered with irritation. "No, I didn't tell him anything about that. Will you just let it go now?"

Her voice drops an octave. "Are you going to do something stupid?"

There's an edge to my response. "What the hell does that mean?"

She whispers like a child. "Try to blow your brains out again?"

I flip. Why can't she let it go? "Trust me, this time if I did, I'd make sure to hold the trigger a little farther back. Don't want to knock out my hearing as well. Hang on, scratch that. Maybe, yes. Then I don't have to listen to you carry on at me about every single fucking thing I've ever done wrong and apparently, still do. Do you think I don't know how spectacularly I blew everything? And for what? For what? So I can be a prisoner here? I wish I'd got it right the first time. Then I wouldn't be here at all. I'd be dead."

My mother's voice quivers. "Don't say that. You're not a prisoner. You're just upset because you saw him, and I would be too, if it were me."

"But it wasn't you." I make a long, loud, exaggerated sigh to calm myself down. "When's Mike coming to fetch you?"

My mother's voice shifts gear. "Any second now."

A beat. "Do I have to be worried? Is he going to come back here? I don't want him causing any more trouble."

My teeth grit hard as I bite back my anger. "He won't be any more trouble."

"Good. No more military men. They're just…bad news."

"Yes." Chase doesn't feel like bad news. But I can't trust myself, can I? I resisted Brock for as long as I could, unable to identify between shaky lust and solid romance. I'd been wrong. With all my training, I should have known how to shoot to kill. But I couldn't even do that. My intuition let me down. *Trust me, Chase, I know you better than you realize.*

Her cell phone rings. She lets it ring some before she answers—she doesn't want to appear too keen. Then in a voice that's high and girlish, she breathes, "I'll be right down."

I can imagine her smile.

She drops a peck on my cheek. "Be safe now, my girl."

"Always." That shouldn't be a problem. In all of the training to be prepared, to scan, survey, weigh up your surroundings, check your exit points, size up potential hostiles, it never occurred to me that I was my own biggest danger.

As soon as she's gone, I slam my bedroom door behind me—a loud, satisfying slam that resembles my anger—throw the crutches onto the floor, and scream. Scream until my lungs bleed dry into my throat. Does she really think I don't relive what happened over and over again? Does she really think that this is what I wanted? God alive. I wanted out. Period. End of. Finish with the whole living thing.

That downward spiral got me. It wrapped me in its black vines of hopelessness and pulled tight until I grew limp, and then it sucked every last bit of life out of me. Every day, I wore cement boots as I dragged through my chores, each and every small action, a Herculean task. She has no idea how it is to be confronted with Mount Everest every morning and told to climb with no pack, no boots, no sunshine in the sky, no helpful Sherpa who speaks your language. Just me, the icy cold, the death grip, and the impossible task.

The only difference between then and now is that I really can't see where I'm going.

Does she know how many times I've walked up those six flights of stairs and wanted to keep walking the next three, up out onto the roof, and keep walking until I drop off? One quick race to the bottom. Sweet oblivion.

But I don't.

I can't stay here.

I burrow into my duvet, shutting my mother's words out. I can't stay here. This can't be my life, not anymore. Ever since I exited that hospital with a cane in my hand and a bandage around my head, I've lived my life on autopilot, circling around and around in suspension, moving but going nowhere.

Seeing Brock has brought that home with a jolt.

I have to leave. Find a place. Somehow make it work. I observe the thoughts spinning around in my head, observe them coolly, just like Razia and the survivors' group have taught me.

A small semblance of calm creeps in. I have to do this, for myself. Have to find the courage to step out.

And *him*?

A sharp twist in my gut. Who wants someone like me? My scar's jagged fold bears the mark of failure. Always there for everyone to see.

Yet thoughts of him wrap me in a warmth I've never experienced before. His touch, his quiet strength, the space he gives me. *I love you, my girl.* There could be something there. *We came together that time.*

Despite the emotional groundswell filling my belly, there's a fluttering between my legs that still basks in my body's afterglow. I unfolded so completely for him, no questions asked. My bedsprings squeak as I move farther under the duvet. The mattress squishes and squashes, the base beneath hard and unforgiving.

This is my reality—this bed, this room, this apartment, this city. Despair pins me down as I lie down and wait until I can see him.

I'll take what he can give me, and then? And then?

Chapter Eleven

I wait for six as we've arranged. The whole night together. Is it wrong to want to collapse into his arms and be held? For him to soak away the worries that gather on my shoulders?

He opens the door and there's no rushing toward me or opening out.

"Chase?"

"Yeah, I'm here." His tone is weary.

"Are you okay?"

His body turns, the door widens, and he allows me to enter his uncle's apartment. It smells like day-old cooked onions and stewing meat.

I've barely crossed over the threshold when he asks the question, "Why didn't you tell me?" It's accusatory, there's anger.

My hackles are up. "About?"

"That you're military."

"How did you know?" Even as I ask the question, I answer it—he's Special Ops, a Ranger. Only the best.

"The second I saw you with him."

"Oh." I flush at the mention of Brock.

"The way you walked alongside him. Yeah, you're on your crutches, but your posture changed, your shoulders shot back, your head lifted. Had a hunch."

"Does it make a difference?"

He pauses a little too long. "It's not what you did,

138

it's that you didn't tell me. What rank were you? Did you get hurt in the field?" He grips my shoulder. "What am I to you? A diversion from your normal life? A little R and R?"

His words are as rapid as the gunfire in my past. And as damaging. He's ripping holes into what we have. "Why do you say that? You know it's not true."

"Do I? You didn't tell me who you are, who you were." His back must be toward the door that stands open. "I'm guessing you're no longer with them?"

"It just didn't feel…relevant somehow."

"How is it not relevant? Hey, Chase, so you were in Special Ops? Funny coincidence that, I was in…insert appropriate response. But you didn't. You let me carry on about things that you already knew the answers to." He comes up closer to me. "Do you pity me? Is that what all this is about? Do you feel sorry for the loser who has to pick up his uncle's life because he can't seem to swim on his own in the deep end?" His words sneer icy cold. "I don't need anyone's pity. I fucked up and now I'm living my mistake, day in, day out." He turns away from me. "I thought you could understand, that of all the people I've met, you would understand."

I clench the crutches' handles, the pressure in my fingertips pushing against the rubberized wood. "I do understand." I shout at him. I don't mean to, but I do. "It's hard, shit. To want something so much you'd bleed for it, and then have it taken away? Shit, are you kidding me? I know all about that. Fuck, I wrote the book and the guidebook."

"Here's a suggestion then: why don't you share it with me? You've got no problem getting physical and sharing your body, how about you share a little trust? Tell me about yourself, who you are, where you're from, what you want—"

"I didn't want to make the same mistake again."

He paces. Then he stops. "That guy? That guy I saw you with? Was he your mistake?"

I hesitate. "Yes."

"Am I your mistake, too? Am I all of those things your mother said? Am I a deserter? A man who should be ashamed of what he's done to his country? Do you think that? Am I a mistake?"

"No, you're not. You're kind and warm, and you've treated me like I was someone."

"You are someone. Too bad for you, you got caught up with a mistake."

I can barely compute the emotions that spit-fire through me. I recoil at the tone of his voice, the unresolved anger that seems to have found its target, warranted or not, in me. I'm reminded of that first day when I 'saw' his face, the tension in his jaw, the knots in his shoulders, the teeth worn down by grinding. I'd forgotten that. I didn't realize so much of it was directed at himself.

"You are no mistake, Chase Rogan. I was a senior lieutenant, stationed in—"

"Too late."

"No! How can it be too late? I'm here—with you—I want to be with you. What does it matter what I used to be? I'm not military now. I haven't been for over two years now. I never will be again." I wish I could reach for him. Fuck these fucking crutches straight to hell. "I'm so much like you, more than you know. You're right, I know exactly how it feels to be spit out of a system that felt like home. To be tossed out when you were no longer necessary. To try and find your feet again when you had nothing—nothing—left to offer anyone. I know. *I know*." A tear trickles down my cheek and I haven't got the strength left to wipe it away. "Is it wrong to want to forget? To not want to remember anything about that time? To not talk about it? To not look back on it? Instead, hide away somewhere warm where you can be someone else, the you who you are without that baggage?"

I can't do this. I thought I could, but I can't.

Without waiting for his response, I orient myself and click my way back through his door.

****

You know what sucks the most about being blind? I can't just roll out onto the street to the nearest bar. I'd have to memorize a route, mark it out, run it through a couple of times to make sure I had the dips and waves in the sidewalk all mapped down. That's what I did for TJ's, but they don't sell liquor. And I want hard tack, straight up and straight down my gullet. Fuck.

I toy with taking a cab. How could I have snatched defeat from the jaws of victory? Would it have been so bad to tell him? No. Instead, I kept it from him. Sure, he was right to be pissed, I probably would be too. But all that talk about mistakes and his being a pity fuck? Well, that was his shit and fuck all to do with me.

Fuck it.

I've got some bills in my pocket. I swing myself through the hall, out the building's front door, and down to the edge of a sidewalk. This is where it could get risky. Yes, I'll be flagging down a cab, but how do I know for sure? I can't stand here out on the sidewalk all night long.

I gather up my courage in both hands.

"You heading out for a wild Friday night?" I recognize that voice.

"Hey, Angie, you know a bar close by?"

"Other end of the street. Down...I'll walk with you."

Her presence is both a relief and a complication. "Thank you."

She grips my elbow with firm confidence and pivots me around. "Careful here, honey, someone's cracked up the tar. Easy does it."

Whenever I hear that tone, I bite my tongue— Angie doesn't mean me harm. I count the steps as we walk.

"Has it been a tough one?"

I stop so as not to lose my place. "You'd better believe it. The worst."

"Hope it's nothing to do with those hunky guys you keep bringing in?" She sighs. "I've always loved men in uniform. They seem so incorruptible."

I can't help but chortle. Has she added up Brock all wrong or what? "He's not all that, believe me."

"Damn, don't blow my fantasies. I still love the end of that military movie. Sometimes when I'm knee deep in pie orders, I visualize that guy swinging in to pick me up and carry me out of there." She adds, "Then he can do his stripper routine."

"I've never seen that movie."

"You'll love it. Guys with washboard abs, what's not to like?"

Her arm's slipped through and linked with mine and she walks with me in a way I haven't since about third grade. It's casual, easy, friendly. I like it.

"You remind me a lot of my sister."

I nearly lose my place entirely with that comment. "How so? She blind too?"

"No, she's strong."

Angie says it as though it's true. I'm not strong. I've let my demons defeat me time and again.

She shifts me to the right. "Here ya go."

I edge one crutch forward, my makeshift cane.

Angie walks with me. "Hey, I can always join you, if you like?"

I want to cry. I can't even do this alone. I crack. "If you've got time?"

She leads me to the door and holds it open.

A thick warm fug of ale envelops me, the chattering of Friday night already crowded by the beer pumps. People shuffle and jive around each other, and I'm aware how a pinball must go through life. Angie moves me around the floor like a mother hen rounding up her chicks.

With a twist of sugar in her voice, she stops at a booth. "Hey, gents, what say you let us slide in? My lady friend here—" She gestures. I smile. "—needs to rest that ankle."

"Sure, no problem."

There's some shuffling and she slides me into a seat. A table, I'm at a table. I'm near wiped out by the sweet and tang of perfume and aftershave. Shit, and I'm in my usual T-shirt and jeans.

"Where you ladies from?" asks one of the guys who's given up his chair.

"The other corner. How about a beer, Skye? You up for that?"

She moves to stand and another voice interjects, "Let me do that."

Angie is all sugar and lust now. "Why, thank you." A little pat on my knee. "All good?"

The gesture tugs at my tear ducts. How long since I had a drink with the girls? Went out on the town?

"Where you boys all from, then?"

The chitchat carries around me, and when the beer and its buyer return to the table, Angie pumps up the flirty-flirt.

The beer tastes like normality.

"What do you do, Skye?" asks someone called Pete or Jake or Ridge. He's the one who's exchanging meaningful nothings with Angie.

It's the first time anyone's asked me since I left the military. The words are foreign on my lips. "Translation. For embassies, mostly."

"Wow."

There are sounds of approval and I am lifted.

"How many languages?"

"Four."

"Wow, I didn't know that." Angie's voice is in awe. "That's pretty incredible. See, I told you you remind me of my sister." Her hand slaps down on my shoulder and squeezes. "She works for the UN. She speaks French. I should introduce you sometime, you'll get along great."

"That would be nice." It would.

I sip my beer. It's been over two years since I had a beer. As I let Friday night drinks wash over me, I am struck by the black hole that my life has been in the after. No friends. No socializing. No nothing. Only that apartment.

I wouldn't be here if it wasn't for him.

Chase sits on my mind no matter which way I turn it. He's right.

I was wrong.

I should have trusted him enough, what we have, enough to tell him everything. And I didn't. I assumed he was like Brock. He isn't Brock.

Angie calls for another round and this time it's shooters.

I want to head back to him. Tell him I was wrong. Share myself with him as I should have. "Last one." I toss back one shooter then another, the liquid burning as it slides down. Whoops and cries of approval meet me.

"There's that other guy you've been in with."

Angie's voice cuts through me. I turn to where I picture the door is, but for all I know, I'm facing the restrooms. Chase is here? Has he seen me?

"Hey, we're here." Angie's voice ricochets through the throng.

I cringe.

She adds, "Not very friendly, is he?"

"Did he see you?"

"Sure, he waved, then turned back to the bar."

I swallow. "Did he see me?"

"You have a red shirt on, it kinda draws attention." She pats my shoulder. "He's probably just getting a drink and then he'll be over."

I have two options here, maybe three—act like I don't know it's him and head on home, ask Angie to tell me, step-by-step what he does, or ask Angie to walk me over to him. Fuck. Two aren't even viable options. I gather up my crutches.

There's nothing easy about my trying to leave. I smack too hard against the table and drinks slosh. "Sorry, I'm sorry, Angie, I have to go."

"We just got here."

I'm on my feet, all ready to move with no idea of which direction. "You stay, Angie. I'm just not feeling well." The white noise of Friday night drinks belies the panic that's roaring through me. Did he come looking for me? No, he's probably doing the same thing I am—searching for oblivion in chemicals.

"Hi, Skye."

It's him. My mouth dries.

"Join us."

Angie's voice rings through me. His arm slides around my waist, and I exhale.

"Next time."

The men at the table aren't unhappy at that decision.

The sudden camaraderie of their response is similar to the warmth that's spreading through me, unchecked.

He came to me. *He's still here.*

It's time.

Chapter Twelve

"I'm going to tell you about my scar."

We're back in Chase's borrowed apartment.

He strokes my hair away from my face. He smells of the beer he downed before we left. "You don't have to do anything you don't want to."

I nod. "I want to. It's important to me." I take my courage in both hands. "It's important to *us*."

His arms tighten around me, holding me close.

I pause, collecting my fears, ready to scatter them to the wind, come what may. He can't know me as he says he wants to, not without knowing what brought me here. All of it.

"Take all the time you need."

His voice is soft and it carries me.

"I'm not going anywhere."

I breathe in. He doesn't know that. "We never know that. Things change. Things can happen." I lay my head on his chest, and I talk.

"My father was killed in active duty. And as ridiculous as it sounds, I never thought he would be. Somehow, he seemed invincible to me. Like he'd always be there. Always be coming home. Even when his grave sank into the earth, I didn't quite believe it. I was sure he'd burst through the front door shouting 'gotcha!' "

He strokes my hair, my face, my neck, as I talk. It

calms me. The tears scratch, the pain in my throat, my chest, expands. "I never thought he would die." I close my eyes tight as the hurt ricochets through me. Waves and waves of grief that never last as long as I think they will but rip me apart while they do, crash through me, knocking me off-balance. "He left me. Left me with her. I don't know who she sees when she looks at me. Someone who's part of her, someone who doesn't exist? I don't know. But he left me with her. To take care of her. He'd always wanted someone to take care of her. He used to call her fragile. I was the strong one, and she was the one who needed help, someone to look out for her."

My voice gets smaller. "I couldn't be that person. I needed someone. Shit, Chase, I needed someone so much, and the only person who'd ever loved me, some asshole shot dead. It wasn't even the enemy, it was friendly fire. Whoever the fuck came up with that expression needs to be shot, if you'll pardon the expression." I choke on my anger. "There's fuck all friendly about shit that kills people."

"That's when I met Brock. He was in my unit; I was his superior. Don't get me wrong, I know the rules. I've known the rules since I was a kid." I hold him closer, tighter. "I know you because I am you. I wanted to be like my dad. I wanted badges on my uniform. I wanted to be the best I could be. I wanted to fight for my country, all of it, just like you."

He waits as I cry. My words are slow. I'm reminded of the survivors' group, how I go there every week and tell half my story, as if keeping the shame with me will help it disappear.

"I thought Brock loved me. He didn't." I recall the

humiliation of those court proceedings. How visibly my desires were paraded and scorned. How my decisions were belittled and reduced. "Everyone knew what had happened. I couldn't go anywhere without someone pointing me out—the officer who took advantage of a junior and got caught." The next part sticks in my gullet, but I push it through. "He used me to gain information, access, advantage. His career shifted and he hasn't looked back."

I've wet Chase's T-shirt with my tears but still he holds me.

"Why did you see him the other day? You don't owe someone like that anything." There's an anger in his voice that speaks to the need for justice.

"I wanted closure."

"Did you get it?"

"Yes." I lift my hand to my scar, feel the ridge, rub over the mark that will be with me until the day I die. "They were deciding what to do with me. My military career, something that had been who I was, looked to be over. Sometimes the pain got too much. I'd sink so low, so deep, so dark, I thought I'd never get out. And one day, I decided to end it." I half-laugh, half-cry. "Did you know that it's possible to not kill yourself by pointing a gun to your temple? I didn't. I thought it would be one shot and sweet blessed relief, life would be all over. Ha. Haha. Ha. Ha. I blew out my optic nerve. They'd seen it before. So shit, I wasn't the only idiot. Others had woken up in a hospital bed in the dark, sure they'd found the other side, only to find they were still here. I was still here."

He litters my forehead with kisses, soft kisses that soothe me. Just for now, I can believe that he can kiss it better. For this moment. He kisses my scar, a stronger, bolder kiss that tips the tears from my dead eyes.

"The irony of it all is that Dad wanted me to care for her. And she was stuck with me. She reminds me every day how she's stuck with me. How he left her with me. How he left her. How her life has been damaged. How she is abandoned. Her."

He doesn't say anything at first, merely gives me the space to cry. "I'm not letting go of you. I'm not going anywhere." He says those words over and over.

They hold me tight.

For the first time in a long time, I find hope in the ruins of my life. Chase has helped me uncover it.

We lie there for a long while, in the sanctity of his couch. I take his hand and pull him in the direction of his bed. I want to lie with him, know him.

He grips my elbow and steers me softly as if I were made of wafer-thin glass.

I don't want to talk more about me, not who I was, not now. I want it to be about us, about this moment. As he lowers me onto his bed, I pull him toward me, finding his lips and kissing him. He opens his mouth to start up more questions but I fill him with my tongue, my silence.

With Chase, I can be free. In so many ways, he is me. He understands. My mind flits to my mother and the promise I made her. She thinks Chase is a military man who broke the rules and spat on his flag. But he's not that. Brock is that.

He works his hands over my waist and I croon. His hands generate heat like he dipped them in the sun. He slides his hands up under my shirt, his heat containing mine. He's wrong—I'm not military. Not anymore. I no longer identify myself by my rank, my years of service, my deployments.

We slide into a more familiar rhythm that slips off awkward edges. He finds the spots on my neck, my earlobe, that have me raise my hips up toward him in greed. My body is not what it once was. Where it was taut, muscled, ready for anything and everything that was tossed my way, it's now slackened. It's softened, rounded out, and found a level of comfort I would have judged before.

It is not military. There's no room for soft and squashy there.

He massages my breasts, his thumbs grazing my nipples.

It is voluptuous luxury and I sigh out my delight. My trysts with Brock were short, sharp and rigid—noiseless, contained, wary of discovery and detection. Two angular bodies rigid with discipline. With Chase, I am free to cry out in delight, to moan, to shudder, to hang onto him, to curl up into him without someone seeing, someone judging, the threat of discovery perpetual.

When he enters me, I surrender to what this is—we're making love.

It's not about bodies. It's about souls connecting. Why have I struggled so much against this? As he moves inside me, my body surrenders to his. I feel his heart and its tendrils of love extending toward me, finding mine and entwining—a thousand pulses of light and energy. I am fecundity in all of its wide-open glory, receptive to the love, the adoration, that he showers upon me. The more I relax to him, the more I am awash in the great cosmos of life. My skin prickles with voluptuous deliciousness that builds inexorably toward release.

For the first time, I am glad that I am alive. My body beats with something earthy and red. Alive.

I am potential. I am creativity. I am everything. I am nothing.

There is nothing between me and the man above me but acceptance, and it is liberating.

I am free.

Orgasm breaks over me, leaving me breathless, as close to divinity in this lifetime as I will ever be.

His own release pulses life into me. "I love you, Skye."

The words race through me in every language, *ti amo, je t'aime, te amo, I love you*, but they hold back somewhere in my throat and die on my lips.

****

All six floors up I consider the same thing: How delicate and precious is a life, a love, a moment? That morning, I'd woken up with him next to me. Throughout the night, his arms weaved over my hips, over my waist, pulling me into his heat, holding me there. I am loved, I am safe, I am protected. We made love. I flush with silliness. That kapowee-zap-boom explosion of feelings. Catching feelings? I'm down with a full-blown fever.

Je t'aime.

Would it have been so bad to stay a little later? Cuddle with him more? Already, I am drunk on his presence.

Ti amo.

But this time, I will remain with one foot on earth and one in the clouds. This morning is my survivors' group. I cannot forget that the downward spiral's door is always open and the calling of that void is not through with me. It will always be there.

I yank out my front door key and turn it in the lock. It doesn't open. The door stays shut fast. I turn the key again, this time with my weight against the door. Still it doesn't budge. Have I got the wrong door? Wouldn't be the first time. I retrace my steps to the elevator, turn back toward the corridor.

This time I count out loud—one, two, three, four, five, six, seven, careful to keep each pace even with the extra swing of the crutches. I stop at our door and reach over the smooth, plywood. A round lock, yes. A tiny dent under the lock, yes. I slide the key in and turn. Again, the door remains locked.

A cold shiver trickles down my back through the back of my legs to my feet. If the door is latched from the inside…but why would the door be latched? Unless…

My stomach twists. What happencd to Ma's weekend with Mike? No way she could have beat me back here. It's not yet tomorrow. Yet that door is slammed, barred and bolted.

My knuckles are poised, ready to knock. I waver. I should hurry back down the stairs, back to him. And do what? My life—what's left of it—is in this apartment, not down at his. Shit, it's not even his apartment, it's his uncle's.

I take a deep breath and rat-a-tat on the door. No sound. I rap again, faster this time. The minutes drip by. The corridor reeks of someone's last night's dinner, a stench of too much garlic and overdone meat. My ankle's alive with frustration, the itching starting up again.

"Ma, you've left the latch on." I say it sing-song style. "I can't open the door." I press my ear up against the door hopeful for any sign of life within to carry through. But there's nothing. No doors opening, no radio playing, no canned laughter from a TV show in the lounge. Nothing.

I try the key again, wriggling it from left to right and back. The door stays shut.

Another thought lashes at me—maybe she did it on purpose? Would she?

I hammer on the door. "Let me in."

I can't stay out here. My armpits ache where the crutches bite into them. An overwhelming urge to toss them away grips me. If I wasn't stuck on these fucking things, I'd…I'd…I'd.

The latch slides back behind the door. I pull back my temper that's bubbling to the surface. I breathe, I count to ten, I picture fluffy sheep jumping over gates.

The air opens up as the door swings. A mix of perfume and cigarettes drifts over—the apartment's smell. My mother.

"What happened with Mike?"

Her voice cuts through me. "Don't make with the conversation. Where have you been? And don't lie this time. Make sure to give me the whole story."

Tongue-tied, I stand there. "I met up with Angie and went to the bar."

She picks up the end of my T-shirt and tugs. "Who the hell is Angie? You don't have any friends. You were with that shithead, Brock, am I right? He arrives here and you just run along again, just like that." She clicks her fingers together "If you think you're setting foot in here again, you're very much mistaken." Her body bars the doorway.

The reek of alcohol zigzags toward me. It fuels the burning that's swiftly rising in me. "I did not meet with Brock. Why would I do that?"

"You did so the other day. And I remember how you were about that sonofabitch."

I grit my teeth and aim the crutches forward across the threshold. "Ma, I'm thirty-five years old."

She pushes back. "And you live in my home. You eat my food, shit in my toilet, and sleep in my bed."

I battle to keep my voice steady. "My life is *my* life. It's not much but it's mine." Every attempt I make to push into the apartment is body blocked.

My mother's voice is so sour it could be bottled as vinegar. "So long as you live under my roof, it's my business what you do. I've had to make huge allowances for you. Do you think it's easy?"

"No, I don't. I never asked you to—"

"Who do you think is going to look after you after what you did? Brock? He doesn't give a fuck about you." She clicks her tongue against the roof of her mouth. "You haven't even got your shirt on the right way round. I can't believe you."

"For the last time, it wasn't Brock." I switch tactics. "Can I come in now? Everyone can hear us out here."

"Ha! Let them. Everyone knows about my useless daughter who blew every opportunity she had."

"It's enough, Ma." My body aches; my ankle aches, my shoulders ache, my soul aches. "I can't spend the rest of my life apologizing for my mistakes. You've made mistakes, too." This time when I force myself into the apartment, she relents. I can't stay here. I can't.

"Aha." She sneers. "It's that other guy. The deserter. That's who you've been screwing around with. What is wrong with you? How many military guys have to break your heart before you get it?"

"I'm tired, Ma." I walk away from her. I can't stay with her.

The phone rings.

She answers, all fresh and sassy. "It's the doctor—for you."

Chapter Thirteen

The doctor removes the cast. It's like having a straitjacket removed. I shiver at that thought. Rewind a couple of decades and someone in a white coat may well have rammed me in a permanent straitjacket, all the better to keep me from harming myself. Or others. It's the others they're most worried about. Depression, and any other kinds of mental illness, makes them uncomfortable.

The doctor handles my ankle with medical precision. He rotates the ankle. "How does that feel?"

Naked, exposed. "A little stiff, but okay." Free.

"Might take a while to get used to."

Are you kidding? I reach down and scratch over the skin that hasn't seen light in weeks. "The itching drove me crazy." I scratch like a dog with fleas.

My mother's in the waiting room. I can hear her talking to the receptionist. It's an inane prattle that fills in the wait—weather, the price of groceries, the high cost of rent, the high cost of medical.

The receptionist uh-huhs and ah-hahs in all of the right places.

Does my mother even realize that she's not being listened to?

We suspended hostilities long enough for her to ride with me over here.

I hobble over, the new weight on my foot foreign,

back to the cane that marks my way. I'm literally taking baby steps.

My mother takes my hand and guides me back through to the exit.

"You're so lucky to have your mom here to help you," says a voice in the reception hall.

I don't answer.

"If by lucky, she means not having a job," my mother mutters as we weave our way back through the medical labyrinth. "Or a man." She fills in the obvious about the shortened weekend away. "All men are pigs. All of them."

I exhale long and loud. I can't stay with her.

"That Mike, he bored me to tears. Endless conversation about how he did this and how he did that, he didn't want to pay the bill, wanted to stiff me with it…" Her diatribe continues to her audience of none.

I won't stay with her.

The cab pulls up to our building. My mother takes the money I offer her and pays the driver. She mutters something under her breath, wry, sardonic.

I follow her out of the cab, careful to place my feet as I alight.

Ma pulls me to the side, around an obstruction, my bearings sliding away with the movement. "Some jerk's parked their truck right in the way."

The familiar creak of the building's door as it opens turns my attention away from jerks and trucks. The door remains ajar with no returning creak. "Someone moving out?"

"Looks like it. There's a couch on the sidewalk."

I stretch out my fingers, hoping to connect with the couch. A twist gathers in my stomach. It wouldn't be

Chase, would it? He was there, last night, with me.

My foot, free from its cast, reminds me that this morning I woke with its plaster prison still intact. And yet, now it is free. One phone call can change a life.

My mother still has my hand as she leads me through the furniture that's gathered up, ready to be packed up and shipped off somewhere else. All I can smell is the belching of car fumes.

I keep my tone conversational. "Who is it? Who's moving?"

My mother swears as she negotiates the door that's been rammed open. "No idea." Her pitch rises on the last syllable. She's lying. She knows who it is.

And in that second, I know who it is, too. That twist in my gut goes for the chokehold. It's Chase. Something's happened. And he's leaving.

I stop dead and let go of her hand. "I'll make my own way up."

"And break your ankle again? You've only just got the plaster removed. Sometimes I think you want bad things to happen."

I pull away as she reaches for my hand.

She makes a noise, a cross between a huff and a puff.

Trust me, Ma, one day you'll blow the whole house down.

I step forward, aware that the objects around me are no longer certain. I stretch my arms out in front of me, feeling into the ether. The front door is two steps behind me, I know how many steps to his door. But if there're boxes and couches and lampstands…

"What are you doing?" My mother's voice is tired. "You look like a zombie."

My feet connect with something hard. I crouch down, feeling, feeling.

Her voice again. "It's a packing box. A fucking packing box." Then back to the no one. "I don't know why you do this to me. Why don't you just take my hand? But no, be like this, then."

I negotiate past the box, which turns out to be two. "If it pains you so much, take me to him."

"Are you out of your fucking mind? Let him go. He's trash."

I reach another tentative step forward. And another. The space between me and his front door narrows.

"If you go to him, never ever think of coming back to me—you won't be welcome."

I clench and unclench my fists. Somewhere down a passage I can hear the tap-tap-tap of Cherry Jubilee. Stay in your home, little dog. I am done with being one of life's accidents.

"Let's go back upstairs—"

She yanks my hand and pulls me, knocking me off my axis. I anchor myself into that spot, the coordinates of my position etched into my mind. She will not knock me off my course. "Ma, I am going to him. I love him." Her sharp intake of breath is like a slap in the face. "And he loves me."

"Ha! Love? What is that?"

Her words toy with every single anxious thought I've run through my own unreliable mind. "It's what I choose to believe I have with him, what I know I have with him."

"He'll leave you, just like—"

"He's not Brock, and he's not Dad. He's his own man. And he's a good man." My words are quiet, but there is strength in their truth. "There are good men out there."

"If that's what you want, then fine. You can have him. Have him and all his dishonor and drinking, you have him."

She hasn't heard me. She's never heard me. I smack my knee into something solid and pain ricochets through me, but she is relentless.

"After all I've done for you, you throw it away. You make me so angry. You are ungrateful, selfish, spoiled; your father spoiled you."

I battle to walk on my freshly recovered foot, but I trip and fall. Her yank rips me back up off the floor.

"Get up, get up, this is what you wanted. This is all what you wanted."

"Enough." My voice is calmer than it should be.

She stops in her tracks.

I say the words from a space inside me that even she cannot reach. "It is enough. I am done."

Her hand drops mine.

I walk the last few paces to his door, that's open, and step in.

My breathing jagged, I find him in the bathroom, the smell of window cleaner, the squeak of cloth against mirror. "You're leaving?"

"My uncle's not looking good." His voice cracks. "He won't be coming back."

I digest this information. We never speak of him, the uncle who has made our coupling possible. Without him, I would not have met Chase, would not have been able to see clearly. "I'm sorry to hear that."

He stands close to me, his hand finding mine.

His presence soothes my edges, tempers my

anxiety.

"They've already found a replacement." He sighs. "He starts Monday. Means I have to get all my uncle's shit out of here, on the double. And let me tell you, this guy has collected more shit than a magpie."

It's the anger of sadness and I press him closer.

He folds into me. "I'll be out of here today."

The words punch me in my stomach. Today? Somehow, I'd imagined he'd be here, always here, six floors down. And where would I be? Up in my cage, six floors up, swooping down to peck a few hours with him, here and there? "Where will you be going? Back home?"

"That gym...I'll put in an offer, take it or leave it."

I gulp away the panic that's tripping through me, rushing to make him stay, keep him here, have him not leave.

"It will be good to be on my own feet again."

I have no answer to that.

He strokes my hair. "I meant what I said about your coming with me."

My heart beats a skip. Leave? With him?

All of the words tumble out. "What if, but if you, what if we don't, how do we know whether, I'm not sure..." My body tightens, when it's my head—my heart—that needs the focus. "I hardly know you."

"You know me here." He places his hand over my heart. "Anything else, we can fill in the gaps."

"You make it sound so easy."

He softens his voice and I reach up to catch the words.

"You don't have to do anything you don't want to."

Everything in my world sighs into place. This time I'm not alone in the dark. I speak so softly he leans closer. "*Te amo, je t'aime, ti amo.*" I pause. "I love you, too."

And with that, I take a step into the unknown, with him.

Epilogue

Sometimes I swear I can hear her heartbeat. If I put my hands under my navel and switch off the outside noise, there it is. *Da-duff, da-duff, da-duff.* I alternate between the book I'm reading and the life we've created. Both unfold in their own time.

I speak to her every day. My mother.

She's still in that apartment, wishing and hoping for fortune to smile on her and lift her out of the malaise that we built there. She is half-excited that her first grandchild is on the way, half-mortified that she will be known now as Grandma.

I sit out on the porch; the sun's last rays warm on my face as I wait for Chase to return.

He bought the gym, fixed it up, and runs a military-fitness based program that appeals to him and his clients.

At my feet, Lola, my seeing-eye Labrador, snores softly. She has become my eyes and my constant companion—my familiar as I navigate my other world.

The birds sing in the trees each morning, storms trash our fledgling garden, and at night, I can hear the coyotes as they wander through, hunting. Out here, the darkness spiral taps, taps, taps, but I'm less helpless to resist its toxic allure. I still fall, though. It's inevitable.

I have a new group that meets every fortnight. I never miss a meeting.

Chase's truck rolls along the dirt truck as it strolls across the land that we bought.

He stops the truck and calls from the front seat. "How are my two favorite girls?"

The fire that burns for him still smolders—I am as hungry for him as ever. "Peachy, babe."

His footsteps creak on the wooden floorboards as he comes toward me.

I open my arms to his body, my mouth to his kisses, my heart to his love.

When I come up to breathe again, I say what I've said every day since I first said it. "I love you." Whether it's to ward off bad vibes or to guard against ill fortune, I don't know. All I know is that I mean every syllable. *Ti amo, je' t'aime, te amo.*

He hears me in every language.

About the Author

Suzanne Jefferies loves to write romance from contemporary to the downright blush-worthy. Based in Johannesburg, South Africa, she believes regular HEAs help to keep away reality blues. Her novel The Joy of Comfort Eating won the 2016 ROSA Imbali Award for excellence in romance writing, and she won the 2011 Mills & Boon Voice of Africa competition. Thanks to an epic cake addiction, she is chasing a half-marathon PB and another stripe on her BJJ belt. She is a member of the Romance Writers of South Africa (ROSA).

Join her FB group Suzanne's Sinners, Saints & Lovers, follow her on Facebook, Twitter, Instagram, and Bookbub, or…

~*~

Visit Suzanne at
http://suzannejefferies.com

~*~

To chat with Suzanne Jefferies and other Wild Rose Press authors of erotic romance, join us at
www.groups.yahoo.com/group/thewilderroses.

Watched
By Suzanne Jefferies

Newly divorced Professor Evie Brown notices her student Cameron Slade and how attentive he seems, so totally unlike her ex-husband. Cameron is also delicious to look at, all taut body, broad shoulders, and hot eyes. He's forbidden territory, but one late afternoon as she pleasures herself in an empty lecture hall, she looks up to find she's not alone. He's there…watching her.

And then there's Sophie Walker. Ever since Evie met the sensual woman, she's allowed her inhibitions to unreel, one by one. It's Sophie who's been sharing Evie's erotic awakening, Sophie who she yearns for. Or is it?

Also Available
from The Wild Rose Press, Inc.
and major retailers.

Sabrina's Seduction
Love Strictly Tested Book Two
By Anna Hague

Desperate to understand my best friend's choice to be a submissive to her Dom husband, I decide to study BDSM for my Master's thesis in Sociology. The very thought of giving up control terrifies me…until my research takes me to a "play party" and I witness Cameron Terry spanking a sub. The striking Dominant's unassuming power mesmerizes me, exciting me in ways I've never known possible while my sheltered and strict upbringing tells me this new desire is immoral. But when at last I plead for what I crave, I struggle on the edge of fear and bliss. Can I change who I've always believed myself to be?

Thank you for purchasing
this publication of The Wild Rose Press, Inc.

For questions or more
information contact us at
info@thewildrosepress.com.

The Wild Rose Press, Inc.
www.thewildrosepress.com

To visit with authors of
The Wild Rose Press, Inc.
join our yahoo loop at
http://groups.yahoo.com/group/thewildrosepress/